THE MODEST BLACKMAILER

Ginger Banks didn't want to get rich quickly, but he wanted a pension for life. He threatened to reveal secrets from quite ordinary people's pasts, demanding small sums from them to keep quiet. With the help of village gossip and hidden microphones, nobody was safe. The police called him a poor devil, more sinned against than a sinner. Ginger had always been a nonentity and so much wanted to be a man of consequence.

6 000807 05

JT

2 1 JUL 2005	263	326
	1084	
11. OCT 05	106	18. 04. 2023
18. NOV 05.	302	
02. DEC 05	1293	
28. JUN 06.	1446	
	1427	
	1745	
12. JUL 06.		
895	1913	
1093	13 JUN 17.	
19		

Circulating

Stock

IRENE WHITE

◆

THE MODEST BLACKMAILER

Complete and Unabridged

LINFORD
Leicester

First published in Great Britain in 1994

First Linford Edition
published 2000

British Library CIP Data

White, Irene
The modest blackmailer.—Large print ed.—
Linford mystery library
1. Detective and mystery stories
2. Large type books
I. Title
823.9'14 [F]

ISBN 0–7089–5771–4

Published by
F. A. Thorpe (Publishing)
Anstey, Leicestershire

Set by Words & Graphics Ltd.
Anstey, Leicestershire
Printed and bound in Great Britain by
T. J. International Ltd., Padstow, Cornwall

This book is printed on acid-free paper

Mrs Marks
Goes to Hospital

'Thank you, ladies and gentlemen, for your kind words. Let me assure you that the pleasure, nay the satisfaction, is all mine.' The voice boomed through the microphone. 'We are lucky to have Professor Robert Marks loaned to us from Cambridge University, to help in establishing a research and reference department in our library.

'I now name it Ann-Mary Memorial Library in memory of my dear wife. Unfortunately we were not blessed with children, but I know that Ann-Mary would have been happy with my decision to bring knowledge and entertainment into your homes through the library in her name. And especially to encourage students to expand their education and fulfil their ambition in learning.

'I declare this library open for all the

good people of Green Borough. Thank you.'

'That is most appreciated, Mr Archer,' said the mayoress, 'we hope that shortly we will have afternoon story readings in the children's section as well. It would of course be for the younger children.

'I remember my grandmother reading or telling us stories when I was young. Of course they had no television or videos, which are excellent nowadays. But the personal touch has gone somehow. Which I think is a pity.'

Then the mayoress turned to a quiet man at her side. 'Professor Marks, we are very grateful for your assistance too. How much longer will you be able to stay with us?'

'I am afraid that I'll have to leave you by the end of the week. You are well established now. If you need any assistance, you can always reach me by telephone in Cambridge. Good day, ladies and gentlemen.'

Robert Marks felt a little tired going back to his hotel in Green Borough, but all the same he phoned his mother at home in Cambridge. The phone rang for quite some time, but there was no answer. Maybe his mother was in the garden or with one of the neighbours, he thought. I will try later.

Just then the luncheon gong sounded and he went downstairs for his meal. Shortly afterwards he rang his mother again and this time a strange voice answered.

'I want to speak to my mother Mrs Marks. Who are you?'

'Oh, I am sorry, Mr Marks. I am a neighbour, my name is Jay Fletcher. Your mother gave me the keys to your house to collect a nightdress and some other items. She fell down on the pathway and cut her head open. We called an ambulance which has taken her to hospital. She had a few stitches put in and they are keeping her in for observation, in case of concussion.'

'Thank you, Mrs Fletcher, please tell my mother that I will come back and see her, if possible this evening. Give her my love and thank you for your help.'

Robert started packing his suitcase,

made several phone calls cancelling all further engagements and drove straight back to Cambridge.

It was getting dark when he arrived at the hospital. Sister took him straight into the ward and said, 'We have just given your mother a mild sedative, so please do not stay too long with her, she needs a good night's rest. You can see her tomorrow of course, and Dr Wentworth would like to see you as well in the morning.'

Robert went quietly to his mother's bedside. She was half asleep; he kissed her and whispered, 'have a good night, darling, I'll see you in the morning.'

The hospital was about twenty minutes away from their home. The house was in darkness as he walked up the garden path. Unlocking the front door, he carried the suitcases in.

Everything was clean and tidy, his mother was an excellent housewife. Just as he entered the kitchen there was a noise from the garden door. Through the cat flap stalked a beautiful tabby cat. She came straight to him and rubbed herself against his trouser leg. Robert bent down and picked her up.

'Hello, Pusskins, you miss your mummy, too, don't you?'

He stroked her and then set her down again, pouring some milk into a saucer, watching her little pink tongue lapping it up.

There was a note on the kitchen table, saying that the cat had been fed and, if Robert needed anything, to call at Number Twenty-two. It was signed Jay Fletcher.

Robert made himself some tea and cut some sandwiches, took the tray into the front room and settled down to watch television. He had an early night.

Feeling quite refreshed next morning he drove to the hospital. His mother was sitting up in bed. 'How do you feel my dear?' He bent down and kissed her. 'Can I take you home today?'

'Robert, my darling, I am fine, just a little tired. The doctor has done his early morning round and told me he would like to keep me here for a few more days. I feel like a queen being waited on hand

and foot. Will you be able to manage at home by yourself? You could of course eat in a restaurant or, better still, I have been told that they have an excellent canteen here at the hospital. Ah, there is sister.'

'How are you, Mrs Marks?'

'Thank you, sister, I am fine. Just a little tired. It is lovely to have my son here and everybody spoiling me.'

'Mr Wentworth can see you now, Mr Marks, will you come with me please.'

'I will not be long. Mother, you have a little snooze till I come back.'

Robert followed sister to the consulting room.

'Come and sit down, Mr Marks. I read about your part in the new library in Green Borough yesterday.

'Thank you, doctor. Will you be keeping my mother in hospital long?'

'I am afraid I have some bad news for you, Mr Marks. We took some X-rays and did a brain scan on Mrs Marks. Apparently she must have been feeling giddy for some time, might even have suffered some blackouts. Elderly people are inclined to ignore these symptoms or put them down to old age. She is a courageous lady and probably did not want to worry you with her troubles. Have you any relations?'

'No, doctor. My father died just after I was born and my mother did not marry again, so we have only each other.'

'I have asked a brain specialist to come and examine her, but according to the scan report there is little doubt that she has a brain tumour.'

'How long do you think my mother will have? A year? Some months?'

'Let us see what the specialist says. You will stay here in Cambridge until we have his report?'

'Of course, Dr Wentworth, and thank you for all your help.'

Robert went back to his mother who was fast asleep and sat down in a chair by her bed. How lovely she looked. She was not even sixty years old, her skin had no wrinkles — she might have passed for his older sister . . .

His thoughts went back to his childhood. How well she had always looked after him and how hard she had worked.

He remembered the little teashop which his mother had bought together with a girlfriend. It was run between the two of them. They only had help from a senior schoolgirl at weekends. His mother baked all the scones, tea cakes and pastry herself in the evenings. She was well known and liked by her clients. As a schoolboy he used to help with the washing up, but whenever possible he avoided contact with the customers.

Next to his mother's bed there was a big cheerful lady. 'Hello, Robert!' she said, 'you don't remember me? My name is Jill Barker. I was the dinner lady in your junior school. You always asked for a big helping of potatoes, I can see it did you no harm. You are still as slim as you were as a youngster. I wish I could say the same. I just look at a piece of cake and seem to put on weight without eating it.

'Are you worried about your mum, Robert? She is such a lovely lady, I have known her for over forty years, ever since she came to Cambridge. Her pastries were famous and often the boys at school used to bet who could eat most of her apple turnovers. Many romances started at her teashop. The students loved her, I know because she often gave them some food to take home without charging for it, knowing how hard up and hungry they were. I think she is waking up now.'

'Robert, are you here?'

'Yes, mother, you had a little sleep, how are you feeling?'

'I am all right, my darling, I am only concerned about you. Mrs Fletcher said she would look after our cat while I am here.'

'How is Pusskins?'

'She is fine, mother. I am sure she misses you as much as I do.'

'What did the doctor tell you, Robert?'

'That I have to take good care of you. The best would be if we plan a week's holiday. Maybe we could go to the Lake District? You always liked it there. I shall make some enquiries and let you know about it as soon as I have some details.'

'That would be lovely, Robert. I shall dream about it. Now I'll have a few more minutes catnap.'

Robert went downstairs to the canteen

to have a cup of tea. He did not feel like eating. Then he went back and stayed with his mother till the evening. She slept for hours with short breaks of consciousness.

Sister did the evening round and stopped at her bed.

'Your mother sleeps very peacefully, Mr Marks,' she said. 'She has no pain. I have just been told that the specialist will be here tomorrow morning. He will see Mrs Marks about ten o'clock. You can see him afterwards. May I suggest a good night's rest for yourself?'

'Thank you, sister, I will follow your advice. I am most grateful for the care you and your staff are giving my mother.'

*   *   *

When Robert opened his front door he saw an envelope on the floor. Picking it up, he went into the kitchen. Pusskins was waiting for him; there was still a little food left in her dish. Mrs Fletcher must have been looking after her. He found a fresh bottle of milk and a loaf of bread in the fridge. On the kitchen table was a bowl of fruit — apples, oranges, pears and bananas. Robert smiled at the kindness of Mrs Fletcher and decided to go round and see her to settle any money which he owed her and say thank you.

First he opened the envelope. A short note said, 'Dear Robert, we just heard about your mother's accident. Please give us a ring when you get home. Is there anything we can do to help? Yours, Rita and Erny.'

He had not thought about them for ages. Erny was an old school friend of his. The last he had heard of him was that he had accepted a chair at Edinburgh University, lecturing in economics. His sister Rita was a nursery teacher in a nearby school. Rita and his mother had often worked together at the charity fetes for the local hospital and several other philanthropic functions. He remembered her as a rather shy young girl.

Well, first of all he had to go round to see Mrs Fletcher.

'Come in, come in,' said Mr Fletcher to Robert's knocking, 'it's nice to see you,

Mr Marks. How is your dear mother?'

'Jay,' he called, 'come down. Mr Marks is here. Would you like a cup of tea or something stronger?'

'No, thank you, Mr Fletcher. Just a word with your good lady.'

'Come into the front room, you must be exhausted.'

'Now then, Mrs Fletcher, how much do I owe you for all the things you have bought for me?'

'There is no hurry for that, my dear, first of all tell us how your mother is? When is she coming home?'

'I do not know, Mrs Fletcher, a specialist will see her tomorrow and then I will know more. At the moment she seems quite cheerful but a little tired.'

He paid Mrs Fletcher and asked her to carry on looking after the cat for the time being. Then he went home and rang Rita.

'How are you and how is Erny?'

'We both are well, thank you. But more important, how is your mother and may I come and visit her?'

'Yes, of course, she would love to see you. Tomorrow the specialist is coming and then I will know more about her condition. Give me a ring in the evening and I will fix a time for your visit.'

'Goodbye, Robert, give your mother my love. We will think of her and wish her better.'

'Thanks, Rita, goodbye.'

Even though Robert was dead tired he could not sleep. Eventually he got up and made himself a cup of tea. There was a strong wind rattling the windows. Some tree branches were knocking against the panes. He could hear Pusskins mewing. She was probably frightened. He stroked her gently.

'We do miss her, don't we,' he whispered quietly. 'I think I will sit in an easy chair and read the paper for a little while.' His eyes kept closing.

* * *

It was nearly nine o'clock when he woke up. A quick shave and a cup of coffee and he was off to the hospital.

The wind had subsided, the air felt fresh and clean. In the wards the nurses were busy washing and tidying up. His mother's bed had been moved near to the door and there was a screen around it.

'Your mother will be ready in a minute, Mr Marks. The specialist has just seen her.' With these words the nurse pulled the curtains back and Robert saw his mother sitting up, smiling at him. 'Hello, Robert, my darling, did you have a good night?' his mother asked. 'I have just seen the specialist and he told me there is nothing to worry about. The tiredness is a natural symptom after the shock of the fall.

'All I have to concentrate on is — getting better. I think by next week you can book us into a nice hotel in the Lake District. Oh, I am so happy, I will try to sleep a little and dream about our holiday.'

Sister beckoned to Robert. 'The specialist can see you now.'

'Sit down, Mr Marks. I am sorry that I have to confirm Dr Wentworth's diagnosis. Your mother is suffering from a brain tumour. She will not be in any pain but will feel more and more tired and will eventually go to sleep — for good.

'I am sure, that if you want to stay with her, we can put her into a side ward and put a lounge chair next to her bed.'

'Yes, please, Dr Phillip. Can you give me any idea how long my mother has got? I will ask at the university for compassionate leave.'

'It might be a few days or hours, Mr Marks, we cannot tell you the exact time, but I would ask for a fortnight's leave, if I were you.'

There was a bit of a commotion at the other end of the ward. Robert heard sister saying rather sharply to somebody behind the screen, 'I told you not to worry Mrs Kendal. She's had a stroke and cannot speak, but she can hear you all right. This is the second time you have upset her. Her pulse is up and I have to ask the doctor to write her up for tranquillisers to keep her calm. Unless she asks to see you, I am afraid that I will not permit you to came into my ward again. If you want any information, Mr Banks, you can see the doctor about it. I have to ask you to leave now. By the way, isn't this Mrs Kendal's shopping bag you are carrying under your arm?'

'No, sister, it is my bag which I lent to Mrs Kendal when she was taken ill, to carry all her things for going into hospital. You see I was in her house fixing her fridge, when she started to feel queer. I called the ambulance and her next-door neighbour came over and packed a few items to take with her. So you see, I am only collecting my own property.'

'Just a moment, Mr Banks, I can see some letters in that bag . . . ' and with these words sister took the bag firmly off Cyril Banks. 'These letters are addressed to Irma Kendal; that means they belong to her. This bag must stay with her unless you can prove that it is yours. I will have to report your actions to the registrar. Goodbye, Mr Banks.'

All Robert could see was a small ginger-haired chap slinking out. He turned back to his mother but she had not heard anything. She was asleep again.

'Fancy seeing that ginger-haired chap here,' said Jill Barker, the lady in the next bed to his mother. 'He is a strange person. I had him in my house once to fix a table lamp and found him snooping amongst my private papers. When I challenged him he said that he had mislaid his screwdriver and was looking for it. He also charged a lot of money for such a simple job. I wonder what he had to do with Mrs Kendal, who is an old age pensioner.'

She beckoned as sister passed. 'Hello, sister, I don't know Mrs Kendal well but I see her sometimes in the supermarket. That most certainly is her own shopping bag. Can the poor dear not tell you that?'

'No, Mrs Barker, Mrs Kendal is paralysed on her right side and cannot talk or move her arm or leg on that side. We are trying to teach her to use her left hand and write things down for us. We might get some movement back at a later stage. Do you know the man who came to see her?'

'Well, I was just saying to Mr Marks that he once fixed a table lamp of mine and charged the earth for it. He was also a rather inquisitive fellow, trying to read my private correspondence. I will not

17

have him in my house again.'

'Thank you for telling me that, Mrs Barker.'

As sister went back to her office, Robert turned round and glanced at his mother. She was fast asleep.

Dr Wentworth looked in and took her pulse. 'It is getting weaker, sister, better have the screens back again please.'

Mrs Marks opened her eyes. 'Robert, you still here? What time is it? What day is it? I feel as if I have been sleeping for weeks. I had such a lovely dream. Do you remember the hotel in Ambleside, the one by the bridge? There was a small river which went straight into Lake Windermere, we stayed there years ago. I dreamt that we gave all our friends a party. It was your birthday and I think you wanted to go fishing and then Erny came, giving you a surprise birthday party. I am not even sure if you were pleased about it.'

'That is right, Mother. By the way, Erny and Rita asked after you. Rita sends her love and wishes you better. I spoke to her last night.'

'She is a lovely girl, Robert. I am very

fond of her. She is kind and generous. I liked working with her and knew her mother quite well. She was a cripple and Rita took care of her.'

The curtain which screened the bed parted. 'I brought you both a cup of tea,' said the nurse coming in. 'You must drink as much as possible, Mrs Marks, to keep your mouth moist. Would you like a biscuit with it?'

'No, thank you, nurse, I am quite happy and contented just lying here and getting thoroughly spoiled.'

'There is a call for you in the office, Mr Marks.'

'Thank you, nurse. I won't be long, Mother.'

Robert lifted the receiver, 'Hello, Robert Marks here.'

'Hello, Robert, this is Rita, how is your mother? I have a free period this morning. Can I come and see her, please?'

'Yes, of course, Rita, she will be very pleased to see you.' Robert went back to his mother. She had dropped off again, looking very peaceful sleeping like a child. Robert went downstairs and bought himself a newspaper. Then he waited at the entrance for Rita.

Ten minutes later he saw her coming along, carrying a bunch of flowers. How nice she looked, he thought, so fresh and unspoiled. They both went upstairs and settled behind the screen, watching his mother.

'She looks so young, Robert.'

'Well, mother married when she was only eighteen. I always thought of her as my elder sister. Would you like a cup of tea?'

'Yes, please.'

As Robert went downstairs to the canteen, Mrs Marks opened her eyes and smiled at Rita. 'How nice to see you, my dear. Where is Robert?'

'He has just gone downstairs to get me a cup of tea.'

'That is nice, now we two can talk just between ourselves. Should I be ill for any length of time, will you look after Robert for me, Rita? I know that you like him a little.'

'Of course, Mrs Marks, but don't worry, you will soon be better yourself and able to take care of him.'

Rita stayed for another ten minutes, had her tea and left. Robert settled down at his mother's bedside, reading the paper and watching her sleep.

Her breathing became more audible. He saw her chest rising and falling for a few minutes and then she gave a little sigh and her breathing stopped.

Robert felt for her pulse; there was none. Quickly he went to sister's office and called her. Sister listened to the heartbeat; there was none.

'I will call Dr Wentworth. Mr Marks, please wait in my office for him.'

Robert sat in sister's office, looking out of the window. Was he dreaming? Everything felt so unreal. Was he in shock? The door opened and Dr Wentworth came in.

'My dear Mr Marks, sorry is such an inadequate word. At least we know that she did not suffer. We can make all the arrangements here from the hospital. Do you know what your mother's wishes were? Did she want a funeral or a cremation?'

'A funeral, Dr Wentworth. I will get in touch with the Reverend Derek Morgan; he is our minister.'

'I am afraid we have to have a post mortem. It won't take long but this is the law. It will be only a few days. In the meantime, you can notify your relations and friends and, of course, your solicitor. If there is anything else we can do for you, please let us know.'

'Thank you, Dr Wentworth. Thank you for all the help you and your staff have given my mother and me.'

★ ★ ★

The funeral was on the following Monday. The Reverend Morgan spoke movingly about Mrs Marks. What a brave little woman she had been, small in stature but a giant in strength and compassion. All who had known her were touched by her friendly and helpful nature.

There were only a few people at the funeral, some old friends of his mother's, some neighbours, Erny and Rita, and a few colleagues from the university.

Mrs Fletcher, as well as Rita, had offered to help but for the moment Robert could not concentrate on anything. The only thing which was real, was the cat, his Pusskins. It kept jumping and rubbing its head on his trouser leg.

Robert Marks' Discovery

The morning after the funeral Robert went to his mother's writing desk. He had never seen it open. There were about ten pigeon holes and a great number of small drawers. Everything was extremely tidy. He glanced at some paid bills, some personal letters from friends. One of the little drawers seemed to stick, as if there were an obstruction somewhere. He pulled at it but it would not budge. Going to the tool box he took out a screwdriver and tried to ease the drawer out. After several attempts it slid open, revealing a small bundle of letters. With a kind of guilty feeling, Robert opened the letters and started reading them.

A picture fell out of a young man and his mother as a young girl. He turned the picture over.

'Staying with Bob at Chalk Farm, 1950,' it said on the back.

His mother must have been about

eighteen years old then, but who was Bob? But somehow the young man looked familiar.

Sitting down by the fireside Robert started reading the letters. They were addressed to 'Dolly' in very affectionate terms. Should he really read them, was it not prying into his mother's life? And yet he could not stop himself. After all it was his life too. Maybe there were some relations somewhere.

One of the letters said:

My darling Dolly,

My parents will not listen to me. My father has given me a thousand pounds and told me to emigrate to America, he does not want to see me again.

I try to appeal to my mother but she won't listen to me. Therefore, I am enclosing a cheque for five hundred for you. That is half of the money I got. I'll work my passage to America and as soon as I am settled over there, I will send you the money for your fare and you will come over too. My darling Dolly, I love you and I want you with me as soon as possible. Look after yourself until we are together again.

Your ever loving Bob.

Robert looked at the photograph again. Somewhere he had seen that young man lately. The question was — where? The picture was about forty years old; that would mean that the man would be about sixty five. He tried to concentrate on the last few months. Where had he been? Suddenly he felt very tired. He closed his eyes and sat down in his favourite easy chair.

A loud ring woke him up. It was the front door. Rita stood outside, smiling at him through the glass panel.

'Sorry to disturb you, Robert. I thought you might need a little help with your mother's things. If I am a nuisance please say so. I can always come at another time if you want me.'

'Not at all, my dear, do come in. I really don't know where to start.

'Have you seen your solicitor, Robert?'

'No, not yet. I rang him up and was told that he is away on holiday and will return next week. In the meantime I am trying to sort through my mother's things. In some ways I hate going through her cupboards. It seems to me so prying. I had a look through her desk and found some rather strange letters. I also found a photo album; would you like to see it?'

'Yes, please. I think that pictures are always so interesting.'

'Also among her letters I came across one special photo and it reminds me of somebody, but I can't think who.'

'Let me see, Robert.' Rita looked at the picture and started smiling. 'You could say that it reminds me of you about fifteen years ago. The hair is different but there is a look around the eyes and the eyebrows which seems an extraordinary likeness.'

'You are right, Rita, how strange. What do you think I should do with my mother's clothes? I also feel that some of her friends might like a small keepsake to remember her by.

'She did not have any costly jewellery. Would you like to choose something for yourself? I am sure my mother would love to know that you are wearing one of her cherished belongings.'

Robert showed her a small jewellery box. Rita picked out a little gold chain and fastened it around her neck.

'Thank you, Robert, that was a kind thought. I shall treasure it always. I will talk to some of her friends and also see matron in the hospital and the ladies who run the charity shops where your mother helped. Wait for a couple of days and I'll let you know what I can find out.'

The next days flew by. The secretary of Salters and Samson rang and Robert fixed an appointment for Wednesday to see his solicitor.

* * *

It was raining heavily. Robert pulled his hat down and leaned against the wind. He felt like the weather, cold and miserable. The rain seemed to bounce back from the pavement.

At least it was warm in the solicitor's office. Mr Samson greeted him kindly and expressed his condolences.

'I have some letters and documents here for you, Mr Marks. Your mother told me to give them to you after her death. She was a lovely lady and we valued her trust. If there is anything we can do for you, please call on us.'

'Thank you, Mr Samson. I am most grateful for your help.'

Robert went home, put a pre-cooked meal in the oven. Carefully he opened the large folder. The first thing was an envelope with the inscription, 'Documents of birth and death'.

His mother's birth certificate read, 'born on the first of May 1932. Dora Marks. Father Arthur Marks, gardener. Mother Betty Marks née Smith.' Then came the death certificates of his grandparents on both sides and his own birth certificate. He looked carefully at these papers. No marriage documents, nothing about his father.

There was another envelope with his

mother's writing on it: 'To my beloved son Robert'. He opened it carefully and began to read.

My darling Robert,

This letter will come to you as a surprise and I hope not as a shock. Bob Archer and I were unofficially engaged. He fell out with his parents and was told that they never wanted to see him again. I believe that Bob had been indiscreet about a business arrangement of his father's, not knowing that one of the competitors was listening in. His father did not want to hear any excuses or explanations but gave him some money and told him to get out of his sight, preferably to another country. Bob tried to talk to his mother and explain things to her but she did not want to hear about it either. In the end he took their advice and sailed to America. We said goodbye to each other and he shared with me the money his father had given him on the condition that he would leave the country. He wrote to me from New York telling me that he was trying to get a work permit. He said something about a green card.

A few weeks after that I felt rather sick in the morning and eventually went to see my doctor. He made some tests and told me that I was pregnant. I wrote to the address Bob had given me but the letter was returned with the words 'addressee unknown'. I did not know what to do. I waited for a while and then my mother found out that I was pregnant. She threw me out, calling me all kinds of names. I was a disgrace to her and her family. Such a thing had never happened before. I was no longer a daughter of hers.

I wrote to a girlfriend of mine who had gone to Cambridge to work in her aunt's teashop. It was called the Copper Kettle. If I wanted I could join them, share a room with Barbara and work in the kitchen. Later on, when the baby came, we could see what arrangements we could make.

I accepted gratefully and went to Cambridge. During the last few weeks of my pregnancy I went to a home for unmarried mothers. And that, my darling, was where you were born. I had tried to get in touch with Bob's parents but was told that I had made a mistake, they had no son.

I wrote to my mother, to ask if there were any letters for me, but there was no answer. I tried to telephone her but as soon as she heard my voice she put the phone down. Even Barbara's aunt tried to get in touch with her for me, to no avail. I missed your father dreadfully but there was nothing I could do. Life was going on. I had to look after you and had to earn a living for both of us. Barbara's aunt became very ill and had to go into a nursing home. She became a permanent invalid and could not go back into her flat. Barbara asked me if I would take over from her and that meant the flat and part of the shop. We worked it out together. Barbara and I ran the Copper Kettle between us. To pay for the flat I did the baking of biscuits, teacakes and pastries in the evening after closing time. We did very well and when Barbara met Freddy and decided to get married, I managed with the help of the bank, to buy her out. I was the then the owner of the Copper Kettle. It helped to pay for your education and of course, being Bob's son, you had inherited his good brain and got some scholarships for the university.

I made some enquiries at the American Embassy but that was also unsuccessful. My darling son, you have been the joy of my life, you never caused me one moment of anxiety. May the good Lord bless you and give you the happiness you so richly deserve. Please God, you will find a partner for life and have a family to be proud of, as I had the privilege and blessing of having you. I want to finish this letter by telling you that you were a wanted child. If circumstances had been different you would have had a wonderful father, who would have loved you as much as I did.

Please forgive me, my fault was that I loved too much.

Your devoted mother
Dora Marks

Robert lifted his head, he had tears in his eyes. How she must have suffered.

There was a strange smell coming from the kitchen. 'Goodness me, my pre-cooked meal.' He had completely forgotten about it. Rushing out into the kitchen he turned off the gas and opened the window. Well, it was not too bad, it had just caught on one side. If he cut the burnt piece off, he could still eat it. Sitting down at the kitchen table, his mind was in a whirl. For years — well, all his life — he had thought of his father as being dead. Maybe he was still alive. In the back of his mind there was something nagging him. Whom could he talk to?

The telephone rang and distracted him. 'Hello, Robert, how are you? I have got the information you asked for.'

'Thank you, Rita do you think you could come round this evening? I have some problems I'd like to talk over with you.'

'Yes, of course, my dear. I'll be with you about eight o'clock.'

Robert lit the fire in the front room and put two glasses out. It was a very comfortable room. His mother had a talent for making it homely.

The grandfather clock had just chimed as Rita arrived. She looked around the room, how cosy it was. The fire was crackling in the grate.

'Sit down, please Rita, and tell me all your news first.'

'All the people I have seen have been most helpful. They will take anything of your mother's you want to give away.'

'That is a relief for me. I nearly forgot, my dear, would you like a glass of sherry?'

'Yes, please, Robert. But now let us talk

about your problem, you sounded quite worried on the phone.'

'I am astounded at some news I have just read. Maybe the best thing I can do is to let you read my mother's letter yourself.'

Rita read the letter and handed it back. 'Thank you for your confidence, Robert. Of course there might be some good news, your father might still be alive somewhere.'

'That is just it, Rita, I think I have met him. I seem to have a mental block somehow, because I can't remember where.'

'Let's go over all the things you have done during the last six months.'

'Right, I'll get my diary and check it out. There seem to be hundreds of people. But wait a minute. A week ago I was asked to help in the establishment of a library in a place called Green Borough. The man who donated it had a slight American intonation and his name was Archer. At least I think so.

'Oh, Rita, my dear, I am completely confused. I think I will have to go and find out for myself. A letter or telephone call won't do. Can I leave everything in your good hands until I come back? Then, having cleared my mind, do you think we could talk about ourselves? Just give me time.'

Bob Archer

The next morning Robert rang the library for Mr Archer's telephone number. He phoned his house and, after exchanging a few pleasantries, he made an appointment to see him the following day.

It was cloudy and the wind was blowing quite strongly. Robert was driving along, his heart was pounding. His hands felt moist and clammy.

Mr Archer opened the door himself. 'My dear Mr Marks, how nice to see you. I do hope that there are no complications with the library?'

'Not at all, Mr Archer, this is a purely private matter as it is of a rather personal nature. Maybe I'd better ask you if your first name is Bob and if you were born in London?'

'Yes, Mr Marks, I was born in London, in a place called Chalk Farm.'

'Would that be a picture of you, Mr Archer?'

Robert leaned over and gave Bob Archer the picture he had in his briefcase.

Bob Archer adjusted his glasses and stared at the photo. 'May I ask how this picture came into your possession?'

'Do you recognise the young lady in the photo?' asked Robert.

'Yes, I do, but you still have not answered my question?'

'This young lady is my mother who died last week. After her funeral our solicitor gave me an envelope which contained this photo and a personal letter to me. I think under the circumstances you had better read the letter yourself, Mr Archer.'

Robert was studying the man as he was reading the letter. He watched the bewildered look on his face. He could hear him breathing hard. There was dead silence followed by a fit of coughing from Mr Archer.

'Please forgive me, I am not as young as I used to be. This has been a very great shock to me. I could do with a drink. Would you like to join me?'

Both men looked at each other. 'My

dear Mr Marks, may I call you Robert? Is your drink all right? Just give me a moment to compose myself. You have brought good and sad news. Let me go back into the past. When I said goodbye to your mother, I thought it would take only a few months until we would be together again. She was my first and only love. I wrote to her regularly but never received an answer. By the letter you've shown me I can only surmise that her mother destroyed all my correspondence.

'I had to leave New York. With the help of some new found friends I went to San Francisco and started work in a dental laboratory. They made plastic dentures. I became an assistant and went to night school. I tried a hundred times to get in touch with Dolly. I sent telegrams, even telephoned her, only to be told that she had moved away and her address was unknown. I tried some friends and also asked my parents to try and find her but she seemed to have vanished. My parents also completely ignored my letters.

'After a few years had passed and I still had no news from her I thought maybe

40

she had found somebody else and forgotten all about me.

'I had no idea that she was pregnant. My poor Dolly, what she must have suffered.'

Bob Archer wiped his eyes and blew his nose. 'Please forgive me, Robert.' He took another drop of whisky. 'I am not really a drinking man. This has upset me quite a bit, but let me continue. A few years later I met my boss's daughter who had come back from Switzerland from a finishing school.

'In a way, she reminded me of your mother, we got engaged and a year later we were married. My boss, Mr Ruben, asked me to open a subsidiary company for him in England. In a way I was glad to come back. I never felt at home in America, the pace was too quick. It was a bit of a rat race.'

'I went first of all to London and found that my parents had died in a fire the previous year. I tried to find Dolly but nobody knew what had happened to her.

'Ann-Mary had never been to England before. We had two weeks' holiday and toured the country. In the end we settled in Green Borough. I opened a manufacturing plant, making plastics and specialising in dentures. I became quite a success and a few years ago I retired. Last year Ann-Mary died and in her memory I donated the library to Green Borough. I had a good life with Ann-Mary but somehow I could never forget my Dolly. She was the great love of my life. Ann-Mary and I could not have any children. She went from one doctor to another but we were unsuccessful. I secretly thought that the fault was mine.

'When I met you for the first time, Robert, when you came to assist us with our library, I felt a great sympathy towards you. Now I can understand it. You reminded me of Dolly.

'Please stay with me for a little while so that we can get to know each other. Or maybe we can make some arrangement to set another date. Do tell me something about yourself. Are you married? Tell me a little about your life?'

'You have to give me a bit of time to

sort myself out. There are quite a few things to arrange after my mother's death. I am glad to know you, I am glad that I came. Certain details have become clearer to me. I will be going back to Cambridge now and will get in touch with you shortly.'

They shook hands and Robert left. Two weeks later Robert received a letter from Bob Archer. It said that he was coming to Cambridge to see somebody at the university and if Robert could find the time, they could lunch together.

Robert agreed, and they both met in a more relaxed state of mind than before.

'I don't know, Robert, if you would like to call me 'father'? What about a compromise and you call me Bob?' They smiled at each other.

'Yes,' answered Robert, 'that would be easier.'

He told Bob all about his job, the house he had shared with his mother for as long as he could remember, his work at the university, his college and friends.

'What about a lady friend?' Bob asked.

'Well, there is Rita, we have become

closer since mother died. Her brother and I were school friends. My mother and Rita used to work together for charity. Rita was one of my mother's younger friends. She was quite fond of her. Rita also came to see my mother in hospital and while I was getting a cup of tea I found them on my return speaking quietly to each other like conspirators. Mother looked positively guilty.'

'Maybe you and Rita could come over to Green Borough for a weekend. I would love to meet her. My house is big enough for you both. We have several guest rooms. My housekeeper does not live in, she comes every day except the weekend. It is often very lonely for me and I would value your company.'

'I will ask Rita about it and let you know, Bob. I could do with a break from everything at the moment.'

Rita Speaks to Ginger
and
Has a Strange Proposal

When Robert told Rita on the phone that Bob Archer was indeed his long lost father she was thrilled.

A few days later, when Robert went to meet Rita, he saw her on the other side of the road, speaking to a young ginger-haired man. He saw her shaking her head and frowning. Robert crossed the road and joined them.

'Hello, Rita, how are you?'

The young man with her gave one hateful look at Robert and turned away.

'What was that all about?' asked Robert, 'What was he doing to you?'

'Oh, he is just a nuisance. He invited me to the pictures, that is the third time now, he will not take 'no' for an answer.'

'Would you like me to speak to him, my dear?'

'No, thank you, Robert, I am sure he will not try again.'

'Bob Archer has been to see me and he was delighted to see my mother's home. He would like to meet you and asked if we would give him the pleasure of spending a weekend with him in Green Borough?'

'Not this weekend, we are taking the local school children on an outing and I volunteered to help. But next weekend I am free, if that's all right with you. I'd love to meet Mr Archer.'

'I will give him a ring and confirm our arrangement then. Have you got time for a cup of coffee?'

'Yes, please, that will be lovely. They have opened a new teashop at the corner. Shall we try it?' They settled in a corner seat and ordered some coffee.

'How long have you known this ginger-haired chap, Rita?'

'Since junior school. He used to follow me around. His father was a drunkard and used to beat him. He lost his mother when he was very young. There's been a lot of tragedy in that family. After the death of his father he came to the orphanage. Later he was apprenticed to an electrician. I don't know if he ever qualified but he seems to have enough money to get by. He is a rather persistent fellow. Once he came to my nursery and picked up one of the little girls. I saw him sliding his hand under her dress. He said it was an accident and he didn't mean the child any harm. He was just fond of children. I am afraid I told him a little lie. I said that you were a very good friend of mine. I hope you don't mind.'

'My dear Rita, I sincerely hope that you spoke the truth. You have been more than a good friend. Would you tell me something? What were you talking about to my mother when I went away to bring you your tea?'

Rita blushed and looked down. 'Your mother asked me to look after you while she was unwell.'

'I thought so. And would you like to do that?' Robert took hold of her hands. 'I never realised what a lonely life I was leading until I met you. I've been so engrossed in my work that I never seem to have time for myself. Only after mother's death and meeting you again I found out that there's something I'm missing. Do you think that you could stand the sight of me for the rest of your life?'

'What a strange way of putting it. Yes, Robert, I think I could manage that.'

He bent down and kissed her hands. 'We will have more time next week. Can we make it an engagement party, when we see Bob Archer? I am not very keen on a big function, just a few friends. What do you think about that, Rita, my dear?'

'I quite agree with you, Robert. So let's keep it a secret for now. I have to go to a meeting tonight but what about tomorrow? I'm free after five that afternoon.'

They met as often as they could and the following week they both went to stay with Robert's father.

★   ★   ★

In the meantime Ginger Banks went home, brooding about the injustice of the world. He had always liked Rita — if he were truthful he really had a crush on her. Now she seemed to have eyes only for that stuck-up fellow from the university. Well, he could not compete with him anyhow. They seemed to be on very intimate terms. He smiled a little. As thick as thieves, he thought. He would show them. If Rita could not be friendly with him, no other man should have her. He followed them several times, furtively noticing their embraces and saw them kissing each other.

He would raise his charges to his customers. A little extortion would do them good. He was really too modest with his fees. Going into the kitchen of his flat he looked through his tool box. All he needed was a battery. In a secondhand shop he picked up a small bracelet. That would do it. He would have liked to have seen Rita's face when she opened the parcel.

He went out and, after buying a battery, he hurried home. Working on the contraption for some time he felt tired. Tomorrow is another day, no hurry, he grinned to himself.

Mrs Fletcher had asked him to fix her bell at the front door. It was only a loose wire, but Ginger took his time. After all, these people could pay for it. He fiddled about for a while and then went into her kitchen where a cup of tea was waiting for him.

'Have you heard, Ginger, that our Rita has become engaged? Isn't it lovely? They are very well suited to each other.'

Ginger nearly choked on his tea. With a tremendous effort he regained control over his feelings. 'That will be ten pounds fifty, Mrs Fletcher, including VAT.'

'That is quite a bit of money, Ginger.'

'Yes, I know, but times are hard and my landlady has raised my rent again.'

Ginger went home quite thoughtful. He'd better hurry up now. A few hours later he stood outside the nursery. It took some time before all the children were collected and at last Rita came out.

'I won't keep you, Rita. I just heard that you got engaged. I wanted to congratulate you and I brought you a small present to show you that I wish you the best of luck.'

'Thank you, Ginger, that is very kind of you. Please excuse me, but I see my fiancé waiting for me.' Rita went across the road to Robert who bent to kiss her.

'What did that fellow want again, Rita?'

'He just gave me a present and wished me good luck.'

'I don't like you accepting presents from people like that. Look, he has gone into that shop across the road. I saw him get out of that old Mini. Its window is open just enough to push this little parcel back into it. You can always send him a note, saying that your future husband doesn't allow you to take any presents.'

'Oh, Robert, don't you think that is a little stuffy?'

'No, my dear, he is not somebody I'd like you associating with.'

'All right, Robert. To please you I will put it back into his car and drop him a line later on, explaining your wish.'

★　★　★

51

Next morning, Robert picked up the local paper and read the headline: 'Explosion in street. Mr Cyril Banks was killed as his car caught fire and exploded as he was driving. There will be an inquest next week.'

Inspector Howerd and Sergeant Watson

Rita and Robert had just finished dinner when there was a knock on the door.

'Good evening, sir, I'm Detective Inspector Howerd and this is Sergeant Watson. We are making enquiries into the death of Cyril Banks. May we come in please?'

'Of course, of course, do come in. We were just having a cup of coffee after our meal. Would you like to join us?'

'That will be very nice, thank you, sir, we can do with a little refreshment.

'You said that you've come to enquire about Cyril Banks. I am afraid I can't help you, I have only seen him but never talked to him myself. But my fiancée knew him slightly, you can talk to her, she is just bringing the coffee in. As the door opened, Rita came in carrying a coffee pot and cups and saucers.

'Hello, darling. These gentlemen are from the police, making enquiries into Cyril Banks' death.'

'Yes, that was quite a shock when I saw it in the local paper. I only talked to him yesterday.'

'Yes, madam, somebody saw you pushing a small object through his car window. May we ask what that was?'

'Most certainly. Ginger, that was the name we used to call him, gave me a present for my engagement. But my fiancé here would not allow me to accept it. And so I put it back into his car, intending to write him a short note to thank him and explain that Robert was not in favour of letting me receive gifts from people he did not know.'

'You didn't open the parcel? Did Mr Banks tell you what the gift was?'

'No, he only said, 'congratulations on your engagement' and wished me all the best.'

'Has he ever threatened you or threatened to blackmail you on any pretext?'

'No, inspector, there is nothing he

54

could have blackmailed me for. What an idea.' She smiled a little.

'Why do you ask, inspector? Was he a bit of a shady character?'

'Yes, Mr Marks, we went through his flat and found letters of a blackmailing activity. He seemed to have a talent for finding out those things some people would not like the world to know about.'

'What we are most interested in is the way he died. Blackmailers seldom die a natural death. We have a number of people who paid him regularly. We are following all the names on the list. Your name was not on it but somebody saw you talking to him a few minutes before he drove off, madam. We will let you know the outcome of our enquiries.'

Mr Sing

Next morning the two police officers went to the Chinese restaurant. 'We would like to speak to Mr Sing.'

'Good morning, Mr Sing. We would like your help in our enquiries into the death of Mr Banks. Did you know him?'

'Well, officer, that is a rather involved story. I met Mr Banks a few years ago. He told me that he came from the immigration authorities, making enquiries into illegal immigrants being employed. At that time I had my nephew here who came as a student to England. One of my regular staff fell ill. Kay, my nephew, volunteered to help out in the evenings. Mr Banks told me that the authorities would construe a different interpretation on these matters. But if I would give him a little extra help he would forget all about my nephew. It was difficult enough to get a permit for him as a student and I did not want to

56

spoil his chances at the university.

'Mr Banks was not greedy. I paid him ten pounds a week and gave him an occasional meal. Did I do wrong, officer? I am sorry. In other countries it is quite common to pay for some special dispensation.'

'Not here, Mr Sing, let me assure you, not here. Where is your nephew now?'

'He had to go back to America, as his father became very ill. I doubt if he will come back to England again.'

'Where were you last Wednesday, about twelve o'clock, Mr Sing?'

'Twelve o'clock is my busiest time in the restaurant — we are serving over two hundred meals. I have hardly time to breathe.'

'Thank you, Mr Sing. If you could come to the station tomorrow and sign a statement, that will be all. I don't think there will be any further complications.'

'Thank you very much, gentlemen. May I offer you both some refreshment or one of our well known specialities? Not in the form of a bribe. Just as a thank you for your understanding.'

'No, thank you, Mr Sing, we are on duty. Good day to you. Well, sergeant, we live and learn, don't we? Let's go to our next call.'

Mr Bertram

Mrs Bertha Bell, who lived only two streets away, was not at home. They spoke to one of the neighbours and found that she had gone to visit her daughter who was expecting a baby. Next on their list was a Mr Ken Bertram who worked for the post office. They went to his place of work and asked for permission to interrupt his job for a few minutes. Mr Bertram paled slightly when they asked him if he had known a Mr Banks.

'More as an acquaintance, not a friend,' he said.

'Did you ever give Mr Banks any money?'

'It is a little difficult to talk about it now,' he answered.

'There should be no problem, Mr Bertram. Come to our police station and you can have a private room to tell us all you know about Mr Banks.'

'Thank you, officer. I am on early shift

tomorrow, so I can call on you as soon as I have finished here.'

Next day Ken Bertram called at the local station and saw Inspector Howerd.

'It was about twenty years ago that I went out with a former school friend of mine. We had not seen each other for some time. He asked me if I could keep a packet for him at my flat. It was a present for his girlfriend. His mother, who did not like Christina, was very curious and kept prying through all of his things. He would be very grateful if I could keep that packet till her birthday. I agreed. We had a meal together and that was the end of it. A few weeks later police came to my flat with a search warrant, found the packet which contained drugs and arrested me. I didn't have a clue as to the contents but they did not believe me and I was sentenced and went to prison for a short time. When I came out, I worked as a butcher's boy for some time, but the smell and sight of the meat revolted me. I am a vegetarian, you know. Then I saw that they were looking for staff at the post office and applied for the job. The manager of the butcher's shop gave me a good reference. I was accepted and have been working here for over eight years. My only fault was that I didn't admit that I had been in prison previously. I don't know how Ginger found out about it. He told me he would never mention it to anybody if I could spare him the very modest sum of five pounds a week. He was very hard up and would never increase the sum. What could I do? I liked my job, so I paid him. And I must admit that he never asked for any more money. Will I lose my job now?'

'Well, Mr Bertram, that is not up to me. If you have been telling us the truth, I do not think that you have to worry unduly.'

'By the way, where were you last Wednesday around twelve o'clock?'

'On Wednesdays I am always on early shift at the post office. That means from eight to one.'

'Thank you, Mr Bertram. If you will be kind enough to sign this statement. You will hear from us in due course. I do not think that you have to distress yourself too much.'

'Thank you, inspector. Somehow I feel much easier now that I have talked about it.'

Mrs Rose

The next person to call on was Gitta Rose. Hers was a modern bungalow, standing in a well kept garden.

Inspector Howerd and Sergeant Watson walked to the front door. Before they could ring, the door was opened by an attractive elderly lady.

'I saw you coming down the path,' she exclaimed. 'What can I do for you, gentlemen?'

They both identified themselves and asked if they could come in for a few minutes.

'Please do. Would you like a cup of coffee? I have just baked an apple strudel. My husband is very fond of my Continental baking but there is plenty and you are very welcome to it.'

'That is very kind of you, madam. We are here in an official capacity. Did you know a Mr Cyril Banks, madam?'

Mrs Rose turned quite pale. 'Oh, my

God. What has happened? Yes, of course I knew that little weasel. He came every month to collect what he called his pension. Fifty pounds a month I paid him. I hope he rots in hell. Have I not gone through enough troubles? Next time he comes he can take a running jump at himself. I won't pay any more. You see, I heard from the Red Cross, when my first husband Toby died after a long illness. He had lost his memory after surviving the concentration camp. For years I thought I was a widow. Then I met Michael and after a short engagement we married. I really do not know how that bandit found out.

'He told me a hard luck story and threatened to tell my husband that I married him bigamously. What would you have done, inspector? My husband is a religious man, he would have considered it a sin to marry a woman whose husband was still alive. I fell in love with Michael and we have been so happy ever since. There must always have been a devil lurking somewhere just to see that we don't find too much happiness. I think that I will confess everything to Michael now. We might get married on the quiet in a registry office and then Ginger Banks can go to the devil. How did you find out about all this, inspector?'

'I have to ask you several questions, Mrs Rose. What did you do last Wednesday around twelve o'clock?'

'Oh, that is easy, inspector. I helped out at a bring-and-buy sale for our local charity. We made quite a bit of money I am glad to say. It will all go to the Save the Children Fund. You see, I was too old to have any children. Well, we all do our little bit. Don't you agree, inspector? But now you really must try my apple strudel, I will not take no for an answer. The kettle is just boiling — I won't be a minute.'

With these words Mrs Rose swept out into the kitchen.

Inspector Howerd looked at his sergeant. 'This is hard work, I could hardly get a word in at all. She seems genuine enough. But the more I see of people the more I appreciate my old woman. At least she gives me peace and quiet when I get

home. Have you ever eaten an apple
. . . what did she call it?'

'Yes, sir, on our last holiday in Austria
we had some. I think it is called an apple
strudel. It is a kind of puff pastry with
apples and raisins and I think a few nuts.
It was very tasty.'

'You mean like apple pie?'

'It's similar, you cannot really compare
it. You have to try it.'

The door opened and Mrs Rose
appeared carrying a large tray with a pot
of coffee, cups, saucers and plates and a
silver dish with a pastry on it, still
steaming.

'Well, now, I must admit that this is
really excellent, don't you think so,
sergeant?'

'Yes, sir, I told you all my family
enjoyed it on our last holiday.'

'Can you come tomorrow to our
station, Mrs Rose? We will not keep you
long. All you have to do is sign a
statement. Thank you for our refreshment
and good day to you.'

Mrs Hillman's Story

As they left Mrs Rose, they saw a slim figure hurrying by.

'I think that is Rita Anson, inspector. Shall we catch up with her?

'Yes, let's see if she has any news for us. Hello, Miss Anson, are you in a hurry?'

'Oh, hello. Yes, I'm afraid I am. Ginger's former landlady — a Mrs Hillman — rang me up. She wouldn't tell me on the telephone why she wanted to see me. She said it was private and confidential and very important and that I have to see her right away.'

'Do you think, sergeant, we should join Miss Anson in her mission?'

'No, inspector, I think that she would rather confide her problems to another lady. I am sure that Miss Anson will notify us if there is anything of interest for us in Mrs Hill's story.'

'Yes, of course I will, but now you have to excuse me, please, a college friend of

67

mine is covering for me in school and I
have to take her class in an hour's time.'
Rita Anson left the two policeman quickly
and hurried away.

★ ★ ★

It was after five o'clock when a call came
through to Inspector Howerd.

'Hello, this is Rita Anson. I wish that
Mrs Hillman had told you her story
herself. As it is, I can only give you a
secondhand repeat. It is quite involved
and lengthy. I am rather tired now. Could
you see me tomorrow after school, let's
say about four thirty?'

'Yes, of course, Miss Anson. See you
tomorrow then. Goodbye.'

★ ★ ★

Rita was a little out of breath as she sat
down in the inspector's office the next
day. 'Sorry I am a little late but I had a
rather trying day.

'Mrs Hillman's concern was mainly
about not wasting the police's time. She

68

told me that Ginger came home one day about a year ago and crept past her kitchen door and hurried into his upstairs flat. She called out to him but he was very short with her. He said he was not feeling well and would stay in for a few days. Later on, as she was cleaning the stairs, she found drops of a red colour and thought it could be blood. In the afternoon she went upstairs to bring him the milk and eggs which the milkman had left on the doorsteps. Ginger did not open the door to her but told her to leave everything outside in the corridor.

'It was four to five days afterwards that she heard him going out. It was already dark and he was wearing his sports jacket with the collar turned up. His voice sounded muffled. He said that he had toothache and a cold and was feeling poorly. He refused any offer of help. She felt that he did not want to talk to her.

'A few nights ago, she could not sleep, lying in bed thinking of him. There had been a spate of muggings going on. It was in the local paper. She wondered if he had been in a fight or had been mugged.

Maybe somebody wanted to do him some mischief and set his car on fire. There had been some strange characters in the neighbourhood, she remembered, at that time, passing her house frequently, looking into her windows. She had not been worried by it. There was nothing worth pinching in her house. The television was a very old model and she did not possess any jewellery except her wedding ring. Mrs Hillman kept tossing and turning in her bed. Then she thought of me. She could confide in me. After all, I was another woman and would understand her not wanting to involve the police. And this is more or less the story she told me, inspector. I told her that I thought it only right to notify you of it and eventually she agreed with me.'

'Thank you for coming, Miss Anson. You did quite right. We will investigate it and see Mrs Hillman herself.'

'Well now, sergeant, we better ask the good lady to come to us here. She might be able to identify some of the shady characters who looked into her windows.

We'll send PC Patterson along in a car to collect her.'

★ ★ ★

An hour later, Mrs Hillman was settled in a comfortable chair in the inspector's office, a cup of tea at her elbow. She glanced curiously at the book of photographs in front of her. Some of these pictures of men looked so pleasant, she could not imagine that they were criminals.

'Take your time, Mrs Hillman, we are in no hurry. There are quite a few books to go through.'

'Surely, inspector, this picture of a clergyman must have slipped in by mistake.'

'No, Mrs Hillman, no mistake. This man is a confidence trickster, the disguise as a clergyman is his stock in trade. He goes round collecting money for the poor. Many people are fooled by his appearance and his soft-spoken voice.'

Peggy Hillman kept turning page after page. She suddenly stopped. 'I think this

71

is one of the men who looked into my window. I remember he was smoking a cigarette. He had a rather large nose and I wondered if the smoke would go up his nostrils and make him cough. He saw me looking at him and turned round, saying something to his companion.

'I could not hear what he was saying but his companion was a tall cadaverous looking chap with a bald head. They both left after what sounded like an argument and I never saw them again. It all came back to me last night when I could not sleep.'

'Thank you for your help, Mrs Hillman. I think that the man you pointed out in the photograph is quite a well known chap. He was convicted a few months ago and is, I believe, in prison. We will look into it. Should we require your help again, may we call on you?'

'What kind of help would that be, inspector? I really don't want to be involved with people like that.'

'We might put him up on an identity parade but you need not worry. You will be with us in a dark room, looking through a glass window at a row of men. We will ask you to point out to us the man who looked through your window, if you recognise him. He will not be able to see you. Your name will not come into it at all, so you needn't be afraid.

'Sergeant, you'd better ask PC Patterson to take Mrs Hillman home again.'

'No, thank you, inspector. I want to do some shopping in this district. No, I'd rather walk. Thanks all the same.'

As Mrs Hillman left, Inspector Howerd turned to Sergeant Watson. 'This picture Mrs Hillman pointed out, is of Joe Brett, a well known bully-boy. He has been involved in a protection racket and, I believe, in drugs. We had better get on to the record office and see his file.'

'There is a note here saying that he has been involved in a fight in prison and is now in the prison hospital suffering from several fractures and concussion. I only hope that it has not affected his brain. He is quite capable of pretending that he cannot remember a thing. We might have to see his doctor first of all.'

Sergeant Watson got in touch with the

prison doctor and the report was not very promising. Joe Brett was in an intensive care unit. The examination had not been completed. He had received a knock on the head. His speech was impeded. They were worried about an internal haemor-rhage.

Sergeant Watson passed on the doctor's words in a message to the inspector. 'Sorry about this, there is nothing I can do. Apparently Joe started the fight. It was in the washroom. Somebody took his piece of soap away. Joe lashed out, only this time he had met his match. The other fellow was an amateur boxer, and then the rest of the boys joined in. He fell against some of the washroom fittings and cracked his head open.'

Eddy Tanner

'Right, sergeant, who do we see now? There is an Eddy Tanner on our list, the name seems to ring a bell. Didn't we have somebody with this name in last year for shoplifting? We'd better go back to the station and check this one out. I like to be sure of my facts.'

They both went back and found that Eddy Tanner of 14 Station Road was the same person, with a record as long as your arm. Shoplifting, embezzlement, drunk and disorderly, were only a few of the charges against Eddy Tanner.

'Let's have some lunch first, sergeant, then we'll be fortified to face Mr Tanner. I wonder why he was on Ginger's list? He is quite a slippery customer himself.'

Eddy was in the garden, repairing part of the fence. He did not seem very happy to see two policeman walking up to him.

'Hello, Eddy, doing a bit of work for a change?'

'Good afternoon, inspector. Isn't it a lovely day? Look what some hooligans have done to my fence. You should bring back the birch. Decent citizens cannot live in peace with all this devilry going on.'

'Right, Eddy, do you know a chap called Ginger Banks?'

'Blimey, do I know him, that good-for-nothing, that crook. His mother would turn in her grave if she knew what became of her darling boy. She spoiled him rotten, she did. But then her old man was not much better. He used to beat the living daylights out of her.'

'Did you ever pay Ginger anything?'

'Well, I helped him out a couple of times and look what he did to me.'

'What did he do to you, Eddy?'

'He pinched my girl, the dirty rotter. I was just going steady with Lisa, when he came along. He bribed her with flashing his money about. You know, inspector, women are fickle. They play on your good nature.'

'I think, Eddy, there are so many questions we want to ask you, it might be better if you come with us to the station.'

'You mean to help the police with their enquiries?'

'That is right, Eddy, you will be a great help. We have several burglaries which are unsolved here on our lists. It might be easier going for you, Eddy, if you could admit to some of them. Ginger knew quite a bit about your activities. Did he ever try to involve you in any of his schemes?'

'He tried to, the dirty bastard. He wanted to make some incendiary devices for terrorist activities but I think that the terrorists found him out. He was not that good in his electrical work. I didn't want to have anything to do with them blokes. They frighten the living daylights out of me. Give me a clean job any time, but them strangers, you can't trust them. They can easily use you for blowing up things and you with it and all.'

'Right Eddy, we will leave you with Constable Patterson. He will take a statement of all the things you have told us. We'll see you later.'

Mrs Bell

'I think, sergeant, we'll try Mrs Bertha Bell again, she might be in by now.' And when they reached her home, the inspector was proved right.

'Good afternoon, Mrs Bell. I am Inspector Howerd and this is Sergeant Watson. We are making some enquiries into the death of Mr Cyril Banks. May we come in, please?'

'I am sorry that he has died. Do come in, please. Was it a heart attack? Was he the Mr Banks we called Ginger?'

'Yes, Mrs Bell, I believe he was known by that nickname.'

'I suppose that even people with black hearts can have a heart attack.'

'Why, do you think that Cyril Banks had a black heart, Mrs Bell?'

'Well, he was a blood-sucking so-and-so.'

'Do you read the paper, Mrs Bell?'

'Yes, of course I do.'

'Did you not see that there was a fire and there was an explosion, killing Mr Banks?'

'Good gracious, you mean to say that this Mr Banks was our Ginger? Well, I presume that now he is dead, one should not speak badly of him.'

'Did you ever pay him any money, Mrs Bell?

'Why do you ask, inspector?'

'Because we found a list with some names on it, among them was your name, Mrs Bell. He seemed to have quite a thriving business in blackmailing people.'

'Oh dear, this is a rather involved and lengthy story. After my husband died his brother came to live with me. He had lost his wife a year before and did not want to stay in the old house any more. We get on with each other all right. He mows the lawn and does the heavy work for me and I do the cooking and darning for him. He has his own bedroom and I sleep in the sitting room. You see, inspector, this is a council house and I am not supposed to take in any lodgers. I thought that, if it's the same name, nobody would notice that it wasn't Stan. They both have the same initials and they do look a bit alike. His name is Sam. It even sounds similar.

'I have no idea how Ginger found out about it. Probably in the pub. My husband used to like his pint and I remember he took his brother a few times down the road to the Horse and Waggon. Ginger came to me some time ago, telling me he wished me no harm, but he was very hard up, could I help him with ten pounds per month. He knew that Sam was not my husband. He also knew about the council's strict regulations regarding lodgers. I have only paid him a few times, as I have to manage on my old-age pension.

'The last time he came, I told him straight that if he wanted me to go hungry, that's the only way I could pay him. I must say he was quite decent about it and told me to let him know when I could spare him a small sum. I found him rather pathetic on the whole. I suppose the only way I can keep Sam with me and fulfil the council requirement is to get married to Sam. I wonder what he would think about that? I never thought that at my time of life I would have to get married again. What would you advise me, inspector?'

'Well, madam, I really can't say. You will have to talk it over with your brother-in-law. By the way, where were you last Wednesday about lunchtime?'

'Wednesdays I am always with my daughter. You see, she has two small children to look after and is expecting her third child. Her feet are very swollen and the doctor advised her to rest as much as possible. I go two or three times a week to give her a break and take the two of them for a walk. In that way she has peace and quiet in the house and I feel needed. I wonder what she would say if I got married to Sam?'

'We would like you to come to the police station at your convenience and sign a statement, Mrs Bell. Thank you for your help and being so frank with us. Good day to you.'

Mr J. A. Kershaw

Both officers returned to the station. They were settling down to read the pathologist's report on Cyril Banks when Sergeant Watson glanced out of the window.

'Hello, hello, what have we here?'

A big black limousine had parked in front of the station. A liveried chauffeur opened the car door and a portly gentleman alighted.

He walked slowly to the desk and asked to see the person in charge of the station.

'Yes, sir, Inspector Howerd has just returned. What name may I say?'

'My name is John Andrew Kershaw. I'd like to see the inspector about the coming police charity dance.'

The desk sergeant went into the inspector's office. 'Can you see Mr John Andrew Kershaw, sir, about our charity dance?'

'Did you say John Andrew Kershaw, sergeant?'

'Yes sir.'

'I believe he is on our list from Ginger. I am sure I have seen that name. Ask him to wait one minute. I'd just like to get my facts right. Yes, here we are — J.A. Kershaw. We'll let him talk first and see what he wants, Watson.'

The desk sergeant showed in Mr Kershaw, who shook hands with both officers.

'I am so glad to meet you, inspector, this is a real pleasure. My colleagues and I have got together and decided to support your charity special this year. It is therefore my privilege to hand you our cheque for one thousand pounds for your fund.'

'This is most generous of you, sir. Please convey our deepest thanks to your colleagues and of course to yourself. In these difficult times we lose quite a few officers due to the increasing crime rate. It helps us to look after the widows and orphans of our officers, who have died in the course of their duty. As you are here now, Mr Kershaw, I wonder if you could answer a question?'

'That sounds ominous, inspector. I hope it will not take long, as I have another engagement.'

'It is just that we do not know if there are two J.A. Kershaws?'

'Not that I know of, inspector. Why? Has somebody not paid his taxes? And used my name to get out of it?'

'No, sir, we have a list from a man who died in a car accident last week. A Mr Cyril Banks, known as Ginger.'

'Oh, Old Ginger! Yes I employed him sometimes as a gardener. Was the other driver also killed?'

'There was no other driver, Mr Kershaw. Ginger's car caught fire and exploded. He was killed instantly.'

'I suppose I'd better cancel my next appointment and send my driver home.' This he did and then began his story.

'It is a long story, inspector. It goes back about forty years. My name was not Kershaw. You have, as I can see, found out that Ginger was a blackmailer. I gave him an odd job now and then, and he

84

asked to be pensioned off to the tune of fifty pounds per week. I know that I should have come to you and told you about this extortion but my wife was just going in for an operation and I did not want to upset her.

'About forty two years ago, my father was involved in a car accident. He spent six months in hospital and when he came home he had changed completely. I remember him as a quiet and loving man. After the accident he took to drink and kept beating my mother. He also molested my younger sister. He was a different person. One day I came home from school and found my mother lying on the floor. My father was standing over her and kicking her brutally. I grabbed the kitchen knife and told him to stop it.

'He laughed at me and tried to take the knife from me. We struggled and he suddenly lurched forward right onto the blade I was holding. I only remember my mother screaming and there was blood all over the floor. I was about eleven years old.

'The neighbours and police came and

the next morning there were big headlines in the paper. 'Young boy defends his mother and kills his father'. It was a traumatic time for the whole family. My mother survived only a few more years and I was send to Yorkshire to an aunt of my mother's. Her name was Kershaw and she adopted me.

'A few years ago I went to a teachers' conference. A vicar spoke, saying that education should start at home, that, as it says in the bible 'honour thy father and mother', children should learn from the beginning to respect authority and so on and so forth. Ginger was at that meeting. I believe he had the job of seeing to the hall lighting. I had never met him before and so, when I found him looking at me several times, I took no notice of him.

'Two days later I received a copy of the article which had appeared forty years ago, with a note saying, 'You hypocrite. How would you like to see the same headlines now, saying respectable gentleman killed his father forty years ago? It would complement the vicar's speech in honouring thy father and mother.'

'I don't know where he turned up this old paper. I would have thought that nobody would have recognised me after all these years. I thought I had changed a great deal. I've certainly put on a lot of weight.'

'You should have come to us straight away, Mr Kershaw. We are quite used to dealing with people like Ginger. You as a law-abiding citizen should know that.'

'You are right, inspector, you are quite right. At that time I was under a lot of stress. Things were not going well in the town hall. We had to give several people notice. There were some irregularities and it took time to clarify everything. What would you advise me to do now?'

'Where you in the town hall last Wednesday around lunchtime, Mr Kershaw?'

'Let me just have a look in my diary. One moment, please. Yes, I was in the restaurant having lunch with a few of my colleagues. Is there anything I could do now, inspector? What will happen to Ginger's body? Are there any relations or any living dependents? I know that he was not the best of characters. Yet somehow I always felt a little sorry for him. You might think that is strange, he was such a nonentity. If there are any funeral expenses, let me know. I'll gladly contribute towards them.'

'Thank you, Mr Kershaw, that's very generous of you. Could you please call in tomorrow? Sergeant Watson will write out a statement which you will have to sign.'

'I bid you good day for now, and thank you, inspector.'

Mr Collin Harrison

'You better get a move on, Joe. Mr Dickson will be here soon. Get his car into the forecourt and fill it up with petrol. Better check the Volvo and see if the lights are working. I am going back into the office to do some paper work. I wish we didn't have so many forms to fill in.'

Collin made himself a cup of tea and glanced out of the window. He saw two men approaching Joe and seem to ask him something. Joe pointed in the direction of his office. A minute later there was a knock on his door.

He opened it and asked, 'Can I help you?'

'Are you Mr Collin Harrison?'

'Yes, that is right. If you are looking for a good secondhand car, you have come to the right place. I have just got a new batch in. Real beauties.'

'Well, we might even do that at a later

date. At the moment we are looking into the death of a Mr Cyril Banks who died last Wednesday in his car. You might have read about it in the local paper? We are police officers. I am Inspector Howerd and this is Sergeant Watson. Did you know Mr Banks?'

'Yes, of course. He bought his car from me. I believe it was a Mini and he paid cash for it.'

'Have you any papers of this transaction?'

'Yes, of course. I have to keep all bills of sale for years for income tax inspection.'

'Did he have his car serviced here and did he buy his petrol from you?'

'Let me have a look into my work schedule book. Yes, here we are, we serviced his car about twice a year. He didn't look after it very well. It had quite a few bumps in it.'

'Did he ever ask you for money, Mr Harrison?'

'He did not.'

'Did you know that he was a blackmailer?'

'Why are you asking me all these questions, inspector? I knew Mr Banks only as a customer.'

'Your name, Mr Harrison, was found on the list of the people he blackmailed. I wonder if there is not something else you would like to tell us? We have to make very intensive enquiries into the death of a blackmailer. People like Cyril Banks live on the knowledge of other people's secrets — which sometimes happen in unfortunate circumstances.'

Collin Harrison looked down. 'May we see your work schedule book, please, Mr Harrison. The last time you serviced his car was last week. Did you find anything wrong with it? Did you work on it yourself or did one of your mechanics do the job?'

'No, I did the actual overhaul and Joe only filled her up with petrol.'

'There is no record here of any payment, as you have on the notes of your other clients. Why is that? Mr Harrison?'

'I must have forgotten to put it in.'

'Going back through your book, you seem to have forgotten to put it in all the time. I am not satisfied with your explanations. You will have to come down to the station with us for further questioning.'

'But I am working, inspector. Couldn't I come down later on? It is half-day today and Joe can look after the pumps when the shop is closed.'

'I am sorry, Mr Harrison. You can put a notice up, saying you are temporarily closed.'

★ ★ ★

It was very quiet in the station. Collin Harrison sat opposite the inspector. A constable sat at the back, taking notes.

'Now then, Mr Harrison, I have the feeling, as you didn't give Cyril Banks any money, that you paid him in kind. You did not charge him for the service and he seemed also to get free petrol from you. Am I right?'

'Yes, inspector, you are quite right. He did blackmail me. Some time ago I bought some secondhand cars. All the papers seem to be all right. Some of them

I bought from the owners and took them in exchange for a different car.

'Of course, they had to pay more money but I took the old cars in exchange and gave them a good price for them. Just by chance I found out that some of them were stolen. By that time I had sold the lot. Thinking that it is better to let sleeping dogs lie, I tried to forget all about it.

'That Ginger chap came one day to my garage and threatened to tell the police about my misdeeds. He said he would forget all about it if I let him have a Mini on the cheap and service it regularly. He would also get his petrol in my garage occasionally without paying for it.

'When I told him that this was my livelihood, he just laughed and said that was my hard luck. I never meant him to die, I only loosened the brakes a little to show him that I was also capable of putting pressure on him. If he had driven carefully nothing would have happened to him. You cannot charge me with murder, this was an accident. It couldn't have been anything else. Loosened brakes would never cause a fire.'

'Right. Now, constable, did you get that all down? Then have it typed out in the office and Mr Harrison will have to sign it. Would you like a cup of tea? Mr Harrison.'

Collin Harrison looked bewildered. 'I do not understand you, inspector. Are you not going to arrest me?'

'No, Mr Harrison. As far as we know, Mr Banks died in an explosion. But this is for a higher authority to decide. All I have to ask is that you surrender your passport and promise not to leave the country for the time being.'

'You mean I can go home now?'

'Yes, Mr Harrison. I would advise you that next time anybody tries to blackmail you, get in touch with us. We are very discrete and can sort things out quicker and easier than you.'

'I really don't know what to say. Thank you, inspector. Thank you very much.'

One hour later Collin left the police station. He was warned that dealing in stolen cars might lead to a charge against him. He had better consult a lawyer as soon as possible.

The two officers exchanged glances.

'Have you got the list, sergeant?'

'Yes, inspector. There are quite a few names on here with some little signs behind them. I wonder what they mean?'

'Well, let's see. It's getting rather late. I think we'll call it a day and continue tomorrow morning. I've had enough of misdeeds for one day. See you in the morning, sergeant.'

Mr Charles Denning

'Good morning, Constable Patterson. Please bring me the report of the pathologist on the Banks case. Morning Watson. You know, that apple strudel was so filling, I had to make a special effort to do justice to the steak and kidney pie my old lady made.

'We'd better start with Charles Denning. Twenty-five School Lane. There is a strange mark behind that name. Let's look into our old files. Yes, here it is. C. Denning was found guilty of murdering a paper boy. He was sent to prison but escaped and is believed to have gone to Yugoslavia with his girlfriend Tania Petrovski, who came to England as an au pair. She only stayed four months and left on the thirtieth of June, 1990.

'Her reason for leaving earlier than intended was that her mother was ill and she had to go home to look after her younger brother and sister. A man called

Carl Driver travelled with her on the same plane. We think that Carl Driver was our escaped prisoner Charles Denning. We asked Interpol to investigate the case. The last we heard from them was that a Mr Carl Driver had registered with the police in Bosnia. Since then all contact has been lost.'

'I don't really think that we have to follow that up, sergeant. Let us concentrate on Miss Flemming, a spinster lady. Living as a companion to Lady Frances Chadwell.

Lady Chadwell

It was on the outskirts of Cambridge that Inspector Howerd and Sergeant Watson called next. It was a beautiful day as they drove up through an impressive gate into the grounds of a manor house. Both policeman looked at each other.

'I feel as though we ought to go in by the servants' entrance. It's a most original building. Probably hundreds of years old.'

They walked up a flight of stone steps and came to an imposing portal. It took a few minutes after ringing the bell before a butler opened the door.

'Yes, gentlemen, have you an appointment?' They both produced their identity cards and asked to see Miss Sophie Flemming.

'I am sorry, Miss Flemming is not here any more.'

'Yes, Cornell, who is it?' came a voice from the hall.

'Two gentlemen from the police,

m'lady. They are enquiring after Miss Flemming.'

'Ask them to step in, I might be able to help them. Let us go into the library and send some tea up please, Cornell.'

'Yes, m'lady.'

'Do sit down, gentlemen, and tell me what you want to see my former companion for.'

'We did not want to disturb you, m'lady. We did not know that Miss Flemming had left you, Lady Chadwell.'

'Fiddlesticks, come out with it. What has Sophie done to involve her with the police? She was the most docile and simple person I have ever come across. She wouldn't say boo to a cat.'

'Where is Miss Flemming now, m'lady?'

'You are trying to avoid the subject, inspector. Have some tea first and then I will tell you where you can find her. It must have been about six months ago that I noticed that Sophie Flemming was suffering somehow. I tried my utmost to make her confide in me but to no avail. She grew more and more anxious and in the end it affected her mind. I pensioned her off and the doctor sent her into our local nursing home. Unfortunately she had developed some cancerous growth and that made her very confused. Whatever she has done or knows about I am afraid she will not be able to tell you. But the nursing home is just ten minutes from here, down Bishops Lane.'

'Did Miss Flemming have any visitors who might have upset her or did she show any distress after receiving any letters?'

'It is strange that you should say that, inspector. I did notice that when a young ginger-haired man called and delivered a parcel, she seemed to be very disturbed. When I asked her about it she said that it was from a friend of hers who was very ill and that had distressed her greatly. I did not believe a word of it but I could not persuade her to tell me what was really wrong.

'I wish you luck with your enquiries and if there is anything I can do to help, please let me know. Good day to you, gentlemen.'

Both officers left and went straight to

the nursing home. They saw the matron and asked her permission to interview Miss Flemming. Unfortunately, as Lady Chadwell had indicated, they had no response to any of their questions. After seeing the doctor who was treating Miss Flemming and getting the confirmation that there was no hope of a recovery, Inspector Howerd and Sergeant Watson went back to the station.

'We'd better see who is next on the list, Watson. Let's have a cup of tea first and sort ourselves out.'

Jimmy Turner

'It says here, 'Jimmy Turner, age fifteen'. That must be a schoolboy. I wonder how he got into Ginger's clutches? Here is his home address. One-four-three, Spur Road. We'd better wait till school is over and then go and see what Jimmy boy has to say for himself.'

Later that afternoon they made their way to the address on Ginger's list.

'Good afternoon, madam, is Jimmy at home yet?'

'Yes, he came home five minutes ago. Who are you? And what do you want my Jimmy for?'

'We are police officers, madam. I am Inspector Howerd and this is Sergeant Watson. We just want to ask Jimmy a couple of questions.'

'Nothing to worry about, madam. You are Mrs Turner? Is your husband at home?'

'My husband and I separated nine

102

months ago, inspector. I take full responsibility for Jimmy. Hang on a minute, I'll just call him.'

Jimmy came in from the garden, looking a little pale.

'These officers want to ask you a few questions, my darling. You'd better wash your hands first. I can see you've done some weeding. Won't you sit down please. He will not be long. You see, since my husband left me, Jimmy is my only company. I am a little worried sometimes. I think a boy of his age should have a man to guide him. Still, I'm doing my best and he's such a good boy, so thoughtful and considerate, I couldn't really ask for a better son.'

'Do you think we could have a cup of tea, please, Mrs Turner. My throat is quite dry,' said Inspector Howerd as soon as Jimmy joined them again.

'Of course, inspector, what am I thinking of. I should have offered one straight away.'

'Now then, Jimmy, while your mother is getting the tea, tell us, do you know a Cyril Banks?'

'Yes, inspector, I do but I don't want my mother to know about it. Can I see you privately?'

'Yes, Jimmy, we can arrange that.'

'We have football tomorrow and as I have sprained my ankle I am excused. That means I am free after two.'

'Right, Jimmy come to the station. We can talk about some of your sports activities when your mother comes in. Thank you for the tea, Mrs Turner, that really was a lovely cup. We have all the information from Jimmy for the time being. I was sorry to hear that he had sprained his ankle. Thank you for your help and goodbye.'

★ ★ ★

Next afternoon Jimmy sat in the inspector's office. 'I really do not know where to begin.'

'Take your time, Jimmy. Tell us where you met Cyril Banks first of all?'

'You see, inspector, I am in the last year at my school. It was about eight months ago that we started to smoke cigarettes. I didn't like it at all but all the other boys seem to enjoy it. So I tried again in the lavatory and set the toilet paper alight. None of the other boys gave me away, I think. I really do not know how that chap heard about it. He threatened to inform the headmaster about it unless I helped him. And that would mean a bad mark against me on my school leaving certificate. He didn't want any money, only information about one of those shifty characters who supply some of the boys with drugs.'

'Have you ever thought of taking drugs yourself, Jimmy?'

'No, inspector, no fear, I know what they can do to our bodies. I went to some lectures a few months ago in the town hall. They showed us a video describing how our liver and kidneys are rotting away. It was really offputting.'

'So what information did you give to Mr Banks?'

'Just that I followed that chap to a pub and saw him talking to a number of people. He said that was fine and followed it up from there himself.'

Revelation About the Town Hall

The phone was ringing in the town hall. 'I would like to speak to Mr Kershaw, please. My name is Howerd.'

'I'll put you through, sir.'

'Kershaw speaking,' a voice answered.

'Mr Kershaw, this is Barry Howerd. I'd like to see you as soon as it is convenient. It has nothing to do with the things we talked about at our last meeting.'

'Right, inspector. It is Inspector Howerd, is it not?'

'Yes, sir, it is. I just had an idea that you could shed some light on a matter to do with the town hall.'

'Would you like to meet me in our restaurant for lunch, inspector?'

'No, sir, I would prefer it to be a little more private if possible.'

'Right. There is a nice place in Church Street next to the chemist.'

'We could meet there about twelve-thirty if that is all right with you.'

'Yes, that is fine, thank you. See you later.'

Both men were punctual and settled down, studying the menu. They ate in silence, exchanging only a few non-commital remarks.

'That was an excellent meal, Mr Kershaw, thank you. Let us have some coffee in the lounge. It has more privacy.'

'Now then, inspector, what is on your mind?'

'You mentioned at our last meeting that there were some problems at the town hall.'

'I'm afraid, inspector, that is something I cannot talk about.'

'Oh no, Mr Kershaw, I do not want to pry into it. Last week we had some rewiring done by a firm called Stebbings and Son. I've got talking to them and was told that they also did a rewiring job in the town hall.'

'Yes, that is right inspector, but . . . '

'Let me finish, sir. As it was quite a big job, they engaged outside help and our friend Ginger was employed by them, to lay the wires. They used him like an apprentice for the basic work but did all the connections themselves. Wouldn't it have been possible for Ginger to put some listening devices in at the same time? After all, it was his opportunity to gain access and knowledge of what was going on in the administration of our town hall.'

'You really amaze me, inspector. I would never have dreamed of anything like that but then I know that I am quite old-fashioned. My goodness, we might have accused the wrong people of indiscretion. I must look into this at once. It might solve some rather delicate rumours. I will tell you how it came about. We were thinking of building a bypass around the town. Somehow word does seem to have leaked out about it and the price of land we need shot suddenly up by a hundred per cent. We thought that one of our people had talked about it, maybe not knowing that anybody overheard them.'

'That's also possible of course. If you

like, we can send you one of our experts in bugging devices along and he can check out your conference rooms. Probably it might be best if he checks the whole building. Sometimes the most intimate things are talked over in washrooms.'

'How soon can you arrange for one of your officers to investigate this matter? There might be other people involved as well.'

'I will set things in motion straight away, Mr Kershaw. Thank you again for a lovely meal and, if there is anything worrying you, please contact us. That's what we are here for.'

'I have to thank *you* inspector. You've really made me think that maybe I am getting a little too old for this job. All these modern devices! I cannot keep up with them.'

It was a week later that listening devices were found in most of the rooms fixed near the newly laid wires. Ginger, the blackmailer, had done a very thorough job.

Berny

'There is a strange sign after the name of Berny and no surname. I wonder what that means? No address either but it seems to say 'St Helens' after it. That could mean a church, a place, a school or anything.'

'There is the school of St Helens only ten minutes from here, Watson. Let's see if we can find somebody with the name of Berny there?'

It was raining quite heavily and the sky looked grey and cloudy. Barry Howerd shook himself and turned the collar of his mackintosh up.

'Let's take the car, Watson. We will find a parking place somehow. Otherwise we will be soaked in this weather.'

The school bell was just ringing as they entered the playground. A teacher, who was obviously in charge, looked at them and came forward. 'Can I help you, gentlemen?'

'Yes, please, we would like to see the headmaster.'

'Have you an appointment?'

'No, we are from the police and will only take a few minutes of his time.'

'I will ask the head boy to take you to the headmaster. William, take these two gentlemen to the main office. The secretary will see if the head can see you.'

The secretary looked very efficient. 'The headmaster is at the moment engaged, maybe I can help you?'

'We are making enquiries for our records about a boy named Berny. It might be a wild-goose chase. Have you a boy of that name here in your school?'

The secretary smiled and said, 'We have several boys with the name of Bernard. 'I am not sure if they abbreviate their names, but let us see.'

She went to a large filing cabinet and looked through some papers. 'Well, gentlemen, we have seven boys of that name. What would you like me to do about that?'

'Could we possibly see these boys, maybe two at a time?'

'Of course. We can start with the senior classes. I will ask their teacher to send them down. We have an empty office next door, you could interview the boys in there.' She showed the two officers into a room which housed some large filing cabinets, some chairs and a table.

'Well, Watson, let's hope we find Berny among this batch. I wonder what Ginger wanted from another schoolboy? Now then, here we are.' Two boys had entered the office looking around a little sheepishly.

'Do either of you know a ginger-haired chap?' the inspector asked.

Both of them shook their heads. 'No, sir.' But the taller one seemed to be thinking of something.

'About a month ago, I saw somebody taking to Berny. I think he had ginger hair. It was really carroty in colour.'

'Thank you, boys, you have been most helpful. We better ask the secretary to send Berny to us. Hopefully he is the right one? A few minutes later a small boy entered the office.

'You won't keep me long, please. I

haven't finished my essay. Cor, you are from the police, ain't you? Ginger told me all about you. I hoped that my last job was useful to him, he has not paid me. My mum says that the police is paid from the taxes. Does that mean that I am a civil servant or something? I have kept my word and kept shtumm about it.' The boy looked with big questioning eyes at Inspector Howerd.

'Where did you meet Ginger then, Berny?'

'I saw him for the first time about four months ago. It was at the school playing fields. We had lost to the team from St Christopher's, three to one. They are a rough lot and did not play quite fair. Two of their team pushed me over, they tripped me up and then pretended to help me. I tell you, they held me down, those devils. I had grazed my knee and did not feel too good. Ginger had been watching the game and came over to me. He helped me up and was very decent. He told me that he worked for the secret service. It is only in the regular police force that you have to be tall. People who are short are much more useful for disguising and concealing type of work. That is what he told me and then he asked me if I would like to help him and become a sub-agent.

'He paid me two pounds for any case I brought him. My mum often wondered where I got the money from. I bought her some little things from time to time. She is always hard up, but I never let on that I was working for the secret service.'

'I think, when you have finished school, you'd better call in at our police station. You will be a very important witness and can help us in our enquiries. Thank you, Berny. You had better go now and finish your essay.'

'Can I tell my mum about it all?'

'Yes, Berny, we'd even like your mum or dad to come along with you to the station. By the way, how old are you?'

'I am nearly ten now. I know that I am not very tall but Ginger told me that's best. People often talk in front of children as if we ain't there.'

'We'll see you later on with one of your parents. Off you go now.'

* ★ ★

It was nearly five o'clock, as the doors of the police station let Berny and his parents in. They went up to the desk sergeant and asked for Inspector Howerd.

'Yes, sir, he is expecting you. Take the second door on your right. Where it says interview room. He will be with you in a minute.'

Berny was holding onto his mother's hand. She comforted him. 'Don't be frightened, ducks, Dad will sort it all out for you.'

The door opened and the inspector came in followed by a young police-woman.

'Good afternoon, everybody. I am Inspector Howerd and this is WPC Glennis Evans. You are Mr and Mrs Ade, Berny's parents?'

'Yes, sir, we are his parents but my full name is Adeyemi, I am from Nigeria. People abbreviate my name as it is too long and difficult for them to remember. I am a bus driver and work shift hours, therefore I cannot always keep an eye on

115

my son. I am afraid, that I could not understand him when he told me that he was working for the police.'

'This is a rather involved business, Mr Adeyemi. Your son is most certainly helping us now, but let me start from the beginning.'

It took quite some time for Berny's parents to understand the situation. It seemed unbelievable to them that a blackmailer could use a boy of this age to help him in his wicked pursuit.

'How many reports did you give to Ginger, son? Did you write them down?'

'No, inspector, only their names and addresses as I could not remember them all and Ginger made me tear them up after he had made some notes himself.'

'I was not allowed to keep anything in writing he told me, and his own writing was a funny kind of thing — all dots and dashes. He told me that it was secret police writing.

'Do you remember any of the things you told Ginger? Any names or addresses or what it was all about?'

'One was a Mrs Bell. I remember that

116

because I thought it was a funny name. And another was the bloke in the China restaurant. I've forgotten his name but Ginger said that was a very important problem and he would look straight away into it. He gave me an extra pound for my good work.'

'If you remember anything else will you tell your parents about it? They will let me know. You really are helping the police now. Thank you for coming. If there is anything else to follow, please let us know.'

Sam Golding MRCVS

'Now then, Watson, who is next on our list?'

'I can't quite make it out, sir, it has been crossed out.'

'Let me see.' Inspector Howerd took the list and adjusted his glasses.

'You're right, it is a bit of a problem. I think I have a magnifying glass somewhere in the car. Yes, it seems to be a Mr Sam Golding and there are some letters behind the name, it looks like M. R. C. V. S. Now where have seen these before?'

'I think, sir, that means a veterinary surgeon. I sometimes watch a series on television with my children. 'All Creatures Great and Small' — it's the story of a vet in Yorkshire. I remember that it said on his front door 'Veterinary Surgery, J. Herriot MRCVS'.'

'It's now about eleven. It looks as if we're just outside Cambridge. We'll see what Mr Golding has to say about our Ginger.'

The sun was just breaking through the clouds, making everything look brighter. There was still a nip in the air. A large notice said

Boarding Kennels. Proprietor Sam Golding MRCVS.

Please use side door for surgery.

A young lady opened the door for them and asked, 'Have you an appointment, gentlemen?'

'No, I'm afraid we haven't. We're from the police and would like to see Mr Golding. It is only an enquiry.'

'I'll find out if Mr Golding can see you. Please take a seat.' A minute later she ushered them into a large surgery.

A man rose from behind a desk saying, 'I am Sam Golding, how can I help you?'

'I am Inspector Howerd and this is Sergeant Watson. We're making enquiries about a person called Cyril Banks.'

'Banks, Banks. I don't remember that name. Ursula, can you look into our files to check if we have a person with the name of Banks, please.'

'No, I can't find anybody with that name.'

'Sorry, inspector, I cannot help you. What did he look like?'

Watson pulled an old photograph from his pocket and showed it to the vet.

'Yes, of course I know him, he has ginger hair.' Sam Golding looked at his watch. 'I was just going to have lunch in the little pub down the road. As it is a rather long story, may I invite you both to join me? We could call it a working lunch. You see, my time is rather limited as I am on surgery this afternoon and there are a couple of small operations to be done. I'm on duty at two. That will give me enough time to tell you the story of that little twerp.'

It was one of those old-fashioned pubs with dark oak beams and an open fire. 'I can recommend roast beef and Yorkshire pudding. Everything here is cooked on the premises,' the vet said as they walked in.

'I think we will follow your recommendation, don't you Watson?'

'Yes, sir, there is a very tempting smell

coming from the kitchen.'

All three settled down and tucked into the meal with gusto.

'Now then, let's waste no more time. I'd better tell you the story from the beginning.

'Some time ago I read in one of our professional journals that there was a new breed of dog coming into England from Israel, called Canaan. It is a kind of a Spitz-family dog, about fifty to sixty centimetres in height, weighing between eighteen and twenty five kilos. The bitches come into this country in the last third of their pregnancy. The pups are born in quarantine. As soon as they are weaned, they can come onto the market and the mother is returned to Israel. These puppies quickly adapt to domestic life. They have proved themselves to be an ideal companion watch dog, small and hardy, cheap to feed. They are inexpensive as far as veterinary cost is concerned, they are resourceful and non-biters of humans.

'A few months ago, this ginger-haired chap turned up in my surgery. He had heard that there were some dogs for sale, which had not gone through customs and had not been kept in quarantine on an import licence. He said that he was not fussy and would pay any reasonable sum, if I could get him a dog of that breed. Somehow, what he said didn't ring true. He was a shifty kind of a chap who didn't look at you when he was talking to you.

'I told him straight that there was nothing illegal with the importation of these puppies. They are a new breed and as yet are very rare. They were shown in the Utility Group at Crufts on the thirteenth of February. After all these explanations his interest seemed to subside. He said that he would talk it over with a friend of his and let me know his decision. I impressed on him my doubts that I would be able to get him a Canaan dog. That was the last I saw of him. I don't even know if he told me his name.'

At this moment the restaurant door opened and a man approached their table. 'Hello, Sam, I thought I recognised that voice; and my two friends from the police as well. Don't let me disturb you.'

'Hello, Robert, what brings you to this neck of the woods?'

'I actually came to see you, Sam. I have a patient for you in my car. My cat Pusskins stepped on some glass and has a nasty cut in her paw. She might still have some splinters in it. May I leave her in the surgery for you to have a look at her? Give me a ring and let me know your diagnosis, please. I can collect her tomorrow afternoon, all being well. So sorry to have interrupted you.'

'Oh, just a moment, Mr Marks, we saw your young lady, Rita, yesterday. She has been very helpful to us, I am sure she will tell you all about it herself. We are still enquiring into the death of our friend Ginger.'

'I wish you luck, inspector, I only saw him for a minute when he talked to Rita. He looked a shifty kind of chap, I didn't like the look of him but now that he is dead I feel quite sorry for him. Strange isn't it? I'd better say goodbye to all of you.'

'Now, inspector, you better tell me your side of the story,' said Sam Golding when

Robert had left. 'How did my name come into this? I bet there was something crooked going on. You've really made me curious.'

'Well, sir, a Mr Cyril Banks died a few days ago in an explosion in his car. We visited his home and found some lists of people's names. Yours was among them but it was crossed out. We believe that Cyril Banks was engaged in a little blackmailing activity. Apparently he was unlucky in approaching you, he must have been misinformed. If you had done anything illegal, he would have pressed you for hush money.

'Apart from being an unqualified electrician, blackmail was his main occupation. He seems to have done pretty well for himself. And that is all I can tell you. That was a wonderful meal, Mr Golding, thank you very much. Oh, could you tell us where you were last Wednesday around noon?'

'Well, that is easy, we had a meeting here in the pub, myself and two friends of mine. We were talking about the dangers of rabies. What with the Channel tunnel being nearly finished, there is the danger of foxes coming over from the Continent. We decided to write to the veterinary college about it.

'Can you give me the name of one of your friends.'

'Yes, of course, he is one of our senior vets from Nigeria called Olayinka. He works for the RSPCA. Quite a brilliant chap. Oh, by the way, I do hope you are supporting us in our work to earmark our dog population. I am sure you have heard about — and probably already use — the micro chip. It is much better than the little disk which is attached to a dog's collar. Identity chips can't get lost because they're inserted under the skin. It is a completely painless procedure, the dog doesn't feel anything. At the moment we are contemplating using it for horses and cattle. It would help to identify any stolen animal, especially in race horses. Some owners register the horse under a different name and try to cheat the racing fraternity. It would stop a lot of thieving and misrepresentation. These micro chips are only as big as a grain of rice.

'Now, gentlemen, you have to excuse me, I am due back the surgery. It was nice meeting you. I wish you luck with your enquiries.'

The two officers stood up and shook hands with the vet before he hurried away down the road. Inspector Howerd poured some more coffee. 'I suppose, Watson, we have to thank our Ginger indirectly for meeting Mr Golding and having such a delicious meal. How interesting about this new breed of dogs. What was the name?'

'Canaan, sir, I made a note of it. I think it is one of the few times that our friend Ginger slipped up. I feel I'd like to sleep off that meal right now.'

'Well, I suppose we could have a few minutes of shut-eye in the car. Better return to the station and write up our report.'

A Lucky Find

On the way back to the station the inspector turned to his sergeant and said, 'Do you know, Watson, I have been thinking. Our Ginger didn't have a post office savings' book, he didn't seem to have a bank account or building society account. What did he do with all his money? I think we ought to go over his flat again, maybe we'll find a treasure trove under the floorboards. Let's see if his landlady is in. We'll have a word with her at the same time. Do you remember her name?'

'Yes, sir, it was Hillman, a widowed lady. She has the ground floor flat. It's an old house, very easily converted into two separate flats. The house was semi-detached, built around eighteen ninety. It had a small front garden with a patch of lawn and a few rose bushes along the pathway. Everything seemed to be well kept.'

There was an old-fashioned knocker on the door, but at the side there was a bell push button.

Sergeant Watson just touched the button. A bell sounded loud and clear. Through the window of the front room they could see a light flashing. A minute later the front door was opened by Mrs Hillman herself.

'Come in, gentlemen, do come in. I recognised you through the glass panel. I was wondering if I would see you again. What do you want me to do with Ginger's things? Have you found out if there are any relations or close friends? Not that he had much to leave. I never saw any visitors and he never talked about his private life. I am rather deaf. You probably noticed the flashing light when you rang the bell. Ginger fixed that up for me. He was very good and when the electricity board told me that I had to have my whole house rewired, he did everything himself and only charged me for the material he used. I do miss him, even though he was not very talkative. It was another human being in the house. But

128

there I am, rattling on . . . That comes from being so much on my own, please forgive me. What can I do for you?'

'May we go upstairs, Mrs Hillman? We would like to have another look at Ginger's flat.'

'Yes, of course, would you both like a cup of tea? I have the kettle on the boil, it won't take a minute.'

'Thank you, Mrs Hillman. Could we borrow a small screwdriver from you?'

'Yes, help yourself, the tool box is under the stair cupboard.'

'You know, Watson, Mrs Hillman has given me an idea. Let's unscrew some of the electric fittings, maybe he used his knowledge to hide his treasure in some of the light fittings or behind some pictures. Our chaps have gone over the whole flat with a tooth comb, but then our Ginger was artful. Remember what he did with the bugging devices in the town hall? Let's see if we can find anything.'

'We'll have a jolly good try.'

The flat consisted of a bedroom, sitting room and what one used to call a box room. Also it had a kitchen and a combined bathroom with toilet. There was a small entrance hall and several built-in cupboards. The furniture looked secondhand but solid and everything was clean.

'You'd better get yourself another screwdriver, Watson, we'll start in the bedroom. I'll use the chair and see to the ceiling lights. You can start on the wall fittings.'

'Any luck yet, sir?'

'No nothing so far.'

'Neither have I, but somehow I have a hunch that we are on the right track.'

They tapped all the walls, checked the floorboards and looked into every nook and cranny. The bedroom had a built-in wardrobe. There was a light switch inside, illuminating its contents. Two suits were hanging on a rack and on a hook in the wall there was a dressing gown. Two pairs of shoes completed the contents.

Inspector Howerd bent down.

'Watson, come here and bring your torch. Can you see some white powder on the floor?'

'Yes, it looks like talcum powder.' He

rubbed it between his fingers and smelt it.

'Talcum powder my foot! This is cement. Hand me the screwdriver.'

'Shouldn't we switch off the mains before you start dismantling the switch?'

'Good thinking, Watson, you go and do it. I'll wait for you.'

The switch came out easily enough. Both looked at a cavity, with some fresh cement at the back of it. At least it looked a different colour than the side walls of it.

'Let's have your screwdriver, Watson, it is longer than mine.' Carefully he eased the screwdriver into the back, loosening some cement and a piece of cardboard. A small plastic bag was lying in the gap. Gently he pulled it out.

'Now then, what have we here?' He opened the bag and shook the contents onto the table. The brilliance dazzled them both.

'Blimey, they must be diamonds. Wherever did he get them? They must be worth a fortune.'

'I remember looking at his passport a few days ago. Ginger had made quite a few trips to Holland. I thought maybe he had a girlfriend there but now I can see the reason for his travels.'

They checked the other light switches in the flat and found over a thousand pounds in cash altogether.

'To think that he was nearly a millionaire and lived like a poor man! It seems unbelievable. We'd better take all this straight to the station. I wonder if it wouldn't be better to put it into a bank and ring our superintendent from there? I'd feel better if this went into a more secure place straight away. We'll tidy up here and ring the super from our car and ask him to meet us at the bank.'

They rang up the station and agreed to meet the superintendent at the bank. It took about twenty minutes longer than they anticipated. There was an accident on the way. A bus had mounted the pavement, trying to avoid an old man crossing the street. Two policemen were on guard duty outside the bank. The bank manager was already looking out for them. One constable escorted them in while the other one parked their car in a nearby garage. They went to the manager's office.

Superintendent Patric Gordon greeted them with the words, 'Well done! Whatever gave you the idea to look behind the light switches? That was absolutely brilliant.'

'We have another surprise for you when you get to the station. First of all let us count all the money with the manager, get a receipt for everything and then get it locked away in the vault. I have never seen such beautiful stones in my life. They must be worth a king's ransom.'

Back at the station the superintendent ushered them both into his office. There on the desk stood a large suitcase and a smaller bag.

'Now, we have just done an inventory. Look at it. One evening suit, one grey suit, several trousers with blazer and sports jacket. All made in Savile Row. Silk shirts and ties from Harrods. Handmade shoes, but the best was in the small bag. A real eye opener. Money in different currencies. We found dollars, marks, lire . . . and two different passports.

'One made out to Mr and Mrs Sullivan

with a photo of Ginger and Rita Anson and another one just of Ginger with the name of Mr C. Carter.

'Apart from his underwear, shaving tackle and washing things, there was an interesting small bottle labelled Peroxide, and several types of spectacles. Our friend Cyril Banks was a very thorough worker.

'I wonder how he would have thought to persuade Rita Anson to go away with him and pose as his wife. It must have come as quite a shock for him when he heard that she was going to marry Robert Marks.

'How on earth did you find his luggage, sir?'

'Well, we had our investigating team look through the burnt-out shell of the car. They found a small key in one of the cracks. WPC Evans thought it looked like a key her aunt had given her to collect some luggage from the locker shelves in the Railway Station. We sent her down there and she returned with these two items. It must have been our lucky day.'

'The only question now which remains to be answered is, how did he die? Was it an accident or was it murder? According to his luggage it was most certainly not suicide.'

The Letters

A week later Bob Archer took Rita and Robert to a hotel in the country. He seemed to be well known there. People kept greeting him and exchanging news from the local city.

He shepherded his guests into a little alcove in the dining room. It was just the right place for a private conversation.

'Now then, my dears, I can't tell you how much I have been looking forward to seeing you. There are a hundred and one things I want to know, I ready don't know where to start now. It is so unbelievable that I have suddenly found a son. A wish has come true.'

The waiter came and they gave their order. Robert told a few stories about his work and research at the university. Rita followed with some anecdotes about the children at school. It made them all laugh.

Then Robert said, 'This is really our

engagement dinner. Rita has accepted my proposal of marriage. I am very happy. We wanted you to be the first to know about it. We are a family now. Both of us would prefer a quiet wedding. We thought that you and Rita's brother could be our witnesses.'

'We could invite a few friends round in the evening for drinks. I thought of spending our honeymoon in Paris. I know the city well. But Rita has never been out of England. It would be exiting to show her some other parts of the world. In this way, Bob, you have, as the saying goes, not only found a son but a daughter as well.

'But make no mistake, we are the lucky ones to have found you. I have always longed for a father. All the boys in school had a dad who took care of everything. I watched my poor mother working away, trying to make ends meet. Now that I know what really happened, I blame my grandmother for her inhuman response. I suppose your parents were just as guilty, but then you were a young man. It always seems to be easier for a man to find work.'

'Yes, Robert, you are right. My poor darling Dolly. If only I had known. However what do they say? Out of evil comes good. Maybe Dolly can see us now together, I know she would be happy about it all. I have been so thrilled knowing that I have a son. A few days ago, I went to see my solicitor who is also a personal friend of mine. I told him the whole story in confidence and he drew up a new will for me.'

Rita and Robert stayed for one week with Bob. They got to know and love each other.

★ ★ ★

In the meantime at the police station PC Patterson knocked on the inspector's door.

'Excuse me, sir, the bank manager from next door would like a word with you.'

'Take him into the interview room, constable, I won't be a minute.'

'Sorry to trouble you, inspector, but one of my tellers has just shown me the picture of Mr Banks in our local paper. He knew him as Mr E Sullivan who has an account with us. Will that be of any interest to you?'

'Of great interest indeed, thank you. I'll have a look at his papers, please. They might shed some light on a number of things which have been puzzling me.'

They both went next door to the bank and settled in the manager's office.

'I have E Sullivan's file here for you. On his statements I see that he has changed some money into foreign currency lately. I believe he mentioned that he might go on an extensive holiday. There are also some papers in our vault, but I have no idea what they are. Most people put their last will and testament and valuables into these boxes. Would you like to see them now?'

'Yes, please.'

The manager rang a bell and asked the entering clerk to bring up Mr E. Sullivan's box from the strongroom. The bank manager unlocked it.

'There is a letter here saying 'to whom it may concern'. As this is a police matter now, I think you'd better open it, inspector.'

'I'll take it with me to the station now.

'Would you please sign a receipt that you have taken the letter with you and also that you have seen the contents of the box of the man who signed himself Mr E. Sullivan.'

At the police station the inspector called his sergeant in and told him the bank manager's story.

'I want you to be present when I open and read this letter. Pay attention to everything, as this might be classified as an important document. I will read it out to you. Here goes . . .'

To whom it may concern.

My name is Cyril Banks.

I had a very miserable childhood. My father was an alcoholic. I have never seen him really sober. He used to beat my mother constantly until she could not longer bear it and left him. She died a year later. My father used to beat me also but as I was fairly agile I often managed to avoid him. He was not very steady on his feet and used to stumble about. After his death I was sent to an orphanage and as I grew up the governor of the orphanage sent me to an electrician to learn a trade.

All my life I have been a nonentity. At best people ignored me. Even at work the other apprentices made fun of me. I was never good at any kind of games. Maybe the lousy food I had made me into a weakling.

I wanted so much to be a man of importance, a benefactor of humanity. The only thing I was really interested in was electricity, but even in that some boy spoiled my examination paper and I failed to qualify.

Some electrical companies employed me as cheap labour. I also did a lot of work mending radios, vacuum cleaners and all kinds of household gadgets. People let me into their homes but I

141

always felt as soon as I had finished the job they were glad to see the back of me. During these kinds of jobs I heard a lot of gossip and thought I might try and put that knowledge to good use and try my hand at a little blackmail.

If I get enough money together I might be able to work on an idea of mine. As I do not know what the future will bring, I am writing this all down and I will give you the reason why I am doing this. Last week I was working for a well known company, when somebody put the main switch on while I was working on some wiring. I fell off the ladder, having received a terrific electric shock. It made me think that nobody will know of my invention which I feel would benefit mankind in providing warmth to the old and sick people, to hospitals and nurseries without poluting the atmosphere. I am enclosing the specification of my invention,

It boils down to this: when houses or flats are built they will include in the walls of the building some strips of metal, like a thick foil paper, to which is attached a very low-voltage cable. I have tried it in my kitchen under the tiles and it works well as a cheap heating device. It would even run on a small battery for over a week. I have tried it. Old houses could be adapted to the same plan.

It was necessary to increase my income with a little more blackmailing but these foolish people deserved to be fleeced. In the end they will realise that their indiscretions have helped in the development of my invention.

I have changed my name and intend to go to America where I have been in touch with some experts who showed great interest in my work. I have accumulated a fair bit of cash and will start in a new country with a new identity and money.

Should I be prevented by illness or death I wish that the specification of my invention together with my worldly possessions to be used in promoting this idea of mine.

Maybe in death I will be successful and be remembered as a man of consequence.

Cyril Banks.

'Well, Watson, what do say about this? Our Cyril, or Ginger as we called him, must have had a good streak in him. Poor little devil. I think he was more sinned against than he was sinning.'

* * *

It was on a Sunday evening that Rita and Robert returned. Jay Fletcher had seen to Robert's house and fed Pusskins. There were a number of letters waiting for him on the hall table. Most of them were circulars or bills. There was one letter however with unknown handwriting on it. Robert opened it and read:

You blasted bastard, may you rot in hell. Why did you have to take Rita away from me, the only woman I loved. You who had everything. A loving mother, a secure background, a university education. Why did you have to entice her away and win her affection? She was the only one who ever said a kind word to me. I would have given her heaven on earth. Yes, you can snigger at me. I would have wrapped her in ermine and pearls. I am not a poor man. She could have travelled around the world with me.

I am going to make you suffer. I first thought of killing you, but that would have been too good for you. I want you to live in agony without her. If I cannot have her, you most certainly will not enjoy her company and love. The present I have given her for your engagement contains the latest type of explosive. You can grieve and be without her for the rest of your life, the same as I have to do. Don't try to find me. I will be out of England before this letter reaches you. I have laid my plans very carefully.

I will curse you till the end of my days.

Your deadly enemy
Cyril Banks.

The next morning Robert went to the police station and saw Inspector Howerd.

'I found this letter on my return from Green Borough. I'd like you to read it, sir.'

The inspector settled himself behind his desk and looked at the letter, reading it slowly. He frowned and shook his head.

'What a strange fellow, what a pitiable character.' He glanced at Robert Marks. 'Well, that will be that. I think this will clear up the case of Cyril Banks. It is as good as a confession of intended murder. Poor old Ginger, what a blessing that he never qualified as an electrician. I wonder what the authorities will make of this letter. It will probably be called death by misadventure.'

'What a blessing that his plan misfired,

inspector. I think I won't tell Rita about this letter. She might be upset and in some way blame herself. Maybe she had smiled at him some time ago and he took it for a confirmation of love. I'll never know what fantasies may have gone through Ginger's head.'

'He was really a poor chap,' agreed Inspector Howerd, thinking about the heating invention and wondering if it could really work.

He was such a pathetic modest blackmailer.

THE END

Other titles in the
Linford Mystery Library:

DEATH CALLED AT NIGHT

R. A. Bennett

Jimmy Ellis believes his parents have died in a car crash when as a young boy he is taken to live with relatives in Australia. The years pass happily, then the nightmare comes. Terrifying images flit through his mind in the dark — all through the eyes of a child, a witness to grisly events seventeen years before. He begins to delve into the past, and soon he finds himself on the trail of a double murderer — a murderer who is prepared to kill again.

SEA VENGEANCE

Robert Charles

Chief Officer John Steele was disillusioned with his ship; the *Shantung* was the slowest old tramp on the China Seas, and her Captain was another fading relic. The *Shantung* sailed from Saigon, the port of war-torn Vietnam, and was promptly hi-jacked by the Viet Cong. John Steele, helped by the lovely but unpredictable Evelyn Ryan, gave them a much tougher fight than they had expected, but it was Captain Butcher who exacted a final, terrible vengeance.

THE CALIGARI COMPLEX

Basil Copper

Mike Faraday, the laconic L.A. private investigator, is called in when macabre happenings threaten the Martin-Hannaway Corporation. Fires, accidents and sudden death are involved; one of the partners, James Hannaway, inexplicably fell off a monster crane. Mike is soon entangled in a web of murder, treachery and deceit and through it all a sinister figure flits; something out of a nightmare. Who is hiding beneath the mask of Cesare, the somnambulist? Mike has a tough time finding out.

MIX ME A MURDER

Leo Grex

A drugged girl, a crook with a secret, a doctor with a dubious past, and murder during a shooting affray — described as a 'duel' by the Press — become part of a developing mystery in which a concealed denouement is unravelled only when the last danger threatens. Even then, the drama becomes a race against time and death when Detective Chief Superintendent Gary Bull insists on playing his key role of hostage to danger.

DEAD END IN MAYFAIR

Leonard Gribble

In another Yard case for Commander Anthony Slade, there is blackmail at London's latest night spot. Ruth Graham, a journalist, and Stephen Blaine, a blackmail victim, pit their wits against unusual odds when sudden violence erupts. Then Slade has to direct the 'Met' in a gruelling bout of police work, which involves a drugs gang and a titled master-mind who has developed blackmail into a lucrative practice. The climax to the case is both startling and brutal.

HIRE ME A HEARSE

Piers Marlowe

Whenever Wilma Haven decided to be wayward, she insisted that she was seen to be wayward. So perhaps she was merely being consistent when she hired a hearse before committing suicide, then proceeded to take her time over the act in a very public place. However, Wilma died not from her own act, but by the murderous intent of an unsuspected killer, and Superintendent Frank Drury of Scotland Yard becomes embroiled in his most challenging case ever.